T0078015

WHO LET THE SQUIRRELS OUT?

The 9th Book in the
Squirrel Chronicle series

RON OSTLUND

authorHOUSE®

AuthorHouse™
1663 Liberty Drive
Bloomington, IN 47403
www.authorhouse.com
Phone: 833-262-8899

Published by AuthorHouse 06/16/2022

ISBN: 978-1-6655-6292-8 (sc)
ISBN: 978-1-6655-6291-1 (e)

Print information available on the last page.

Any people depicted in stock imagery provided by Getty Images are models, and such images are being used for illustrative purposes only. Certain stock imagery © Getty Images.

This book is printed on acid-free paper.

Because of the dynamic nature of the Internet, any web addresses or links contained in this book may have changed since publication and may no longer be valid. The views expressed in this work are solely those of the author and do not necessarily reflect the views of the publisher, and the publisher hereby disclaims any responsibility for them.

CONTENTS

IGNORE THE TURKEY IN THE ROOM

Roscoe was cutting across the Clearing when he saw it. He'd been thinking about the agenda for the meeting of the *Committee for the Protection of Neighborhood Resources*, and almost missed the flash of color between the trees and the "Brrck, brrck," that followed. He stepped on the platform and was about to open the door when he realized what he saw was a turkey. He'd seen one in their old neighborhood but not here in the woods. He turned to see if it was still there and bumped into Dorman, a committee member.

When he saw Roscoe step away from the door Dorman asked, "Is the meeting over?" If it had been it wouldn't be the first one he'd missed recently. He'd been one of the more dependable committee members until he moved from his nest in the woods to the senior center. Now when he left for a meeting, someone would ask what was on the agenda. When he told them they'd laugh and say, "That old chestnut? We were kicking that around when I was on the committee." Eventually they'd run out of things to say and wander off, allowing Dorman to leave.

"Did you see that?" Roscoe asked, then remembered Dorman's failing eyesight and quickly added, "Never mind."

"See what?" Dorman asked, looking around the Clearing. "What am I supposed to see?"

"It's nothing," Roscoe said as he opened the door and stepped inside.

Later that morning Webster, the community librarian, ran across the Clearing, up the steps, and tapped on the meeting room door. He saw the *Meeting In Progress Do Nut Disturb* sign on the doorknob and shook his head. He'd pointed out the misspelled word on the sign, but nothing had been done about it. He told himself to forget the sign and remember why he was there.

The sergeant at arms opened the door and eyed him suspiciously before asking, "What?"

"I need to speak to Roscoe. Immediately!" Webster told him with all the authority he was capable of.

"You and half the community, get in line." The sergeant at arms grunted, anxious to get rid of him. This was his first day on the job and he didn't want word to get out that he was a pushover.

Webster looked around, didn't see anyone and asked, "What line?"

The sergeant at arms studied him for a moment before saying, "For a librarian your kind of slow on the uptake. It's a figure of speech. What I'm saying is, you can't see him now. Got it?" He pointed to the meeting in progress sign and told Webster to, "Take a hike." He slammed the door, cutting off the possibility of more questions.

What Webster wanted to tell Roscoe couldn't wait until the meeting was over, they tended to drag on longer than scheduled and they didn't have that much time. He hurried down the steps and around the tree the meeting room is in, planning to climb up and tap on the small window above the wooden bench to get his attention.

He raised a paw and was about to knock on the window when the sergeant at arms saw him, hurried over, and stood with his back to window.

"Hey Webster, what are you doing up there?" Someone called and when he looked, he saw Roscoe walking across the Clearing.

"I thought you were in there," Webster said, pointing to the meeting room.

"I left a page of the budget in my nest and went to get it."

"When you see the sign in fr ont of Seed Mans's building the budget will be the least of your concerns," Webster said as he hurried down the tree and moved toward the path that led out of the woods.

"I'm in a meeting, I can't go anywhere." Roscoe thought he'd made that clear.

"After you've seen the sign in front of Seed Man's building, you'll cancel the meeting. What good is a budget if there's no one here to use it? You have bigger problems to worry about."

Roscoe stood for a moment, trying to decide what to do. This was the final review of a budget they'd worked on for weeks. On the other paw, Webster wasn't the kind of guy who saw every event as an emergency. "This had better be good," Roscoe said as he hurried after him.

They stopped in front of the sign at the entrance to Seed Man's building and Webster asked, "What do you think of that?"

"You know I can't read human markings so I don't know what to think," Roscoe said and braced himself for the usual reminder that, with a little effort, he could. Instead, Webster pointed to each word as he read, "Turkey hunt sponsored by Big G Grocery."

"So?" from Roscoe.

"A turkey hunt Roscoe. In the woods. Our woods." Webster told himself to slow down, he'd had time to think about it, Roscoe hadn't.

Roscoe shook his head. "Seed Man wouldn't do that."

"He's not. Someone named Big G is. The woods will be full of humans with guns hunting a turkey. It's all there in black and white and a little red where they drew an X over the picture of the turkey."

"You're sure that's what it says? You're not making it up?" Roscoe asked knowing there'd be questions when he told the committee. If humans were going to hunt a turkey in the woods, they'd have to act fast and that wasn't something they did very well. It will take weeks to come up with a plan and longer to put it into action. "Does it say when the turkey hunt is?"

Webster nodded and said solemnly, "Saturday. You've got six days to figure out what to do or you can kiss our home in the woods goodbye. If they don't find a turkey, they'll shoot anything that moves."

When they returned to the Clearing, Webster went to the library and Roscoe to the meeting room where he found, other than the sergeant at arms, the room was empty. "Where is everyone?" he asked.

"They waited but when you didn't come back with the missing page, they voted to adjourn. They said they had better things to do than sit around and wait for you." The sergeant at arms shrugged and said he'd be gone too but stayed to straighten things up.

Roscoe told him to, "Get them back for an emergency meeting." When he didn't move, he asked, "What?"

"That wasn't in the job description you gave me. You said I was supposed to keep visitors out and committee members in line. There wasn't anything about bringing them back after they've gone."

"Never mind, I'll do it," Roscoe said and went to his desk to write down everything he could remember about the message on the sign. If he didn't, they'd spend the first part of the meeting arguing over the wording, and the remainder deciding what it meant. He looked up when the sergeant at arms cleared his throat and asked, "Can I go or..." It was his first day on the job and committee members leaving and coming back confused him.

"Yes. Go." Roscoe said and knew if he didn't come up with a plan to save the community before the committee returned their life in the woods would be over.

Roscoe was right about one thing. If Harold Finebender, known to the squirrels in the woods as Seed Man, had anything to say about it, there wouldn't be a turkey hunt and their lives would go on as they had since moving there.

Unfortunately, he didn't.

The *Office Zone*, the company that built the museum to house Otis Tharp's collection of fountain pens, had fallen on hard times. Part of the problem was the economy. Although financial experts said the recession was over, sales at the *Office Zone* remained flat. The management team failed to see the shift from customers shopping in stores, to purchasing thing's online. They were stuck on the idea that a shopper needed to feel the weight of the pen in their hand, decide if they preferred a thick or thin line and select a color that matched what they were wearing or the inside of their briefcase. They missed the new generation of professionals don't care about those things. Their communication was done on mobile phones or laptops, no one took notes by hand anymore. A few used a fountain pen at weddings for those attending to sign a guest book, but most had switched to a member of the bridal party checking names off a spreadsheet on a computer screen.

To keep from losing everything and generate enough cash to keep the doors of their stores open, the board of directors voted to sell the building that housed the museum to George Granger, owner of the Big G grocery chain. He had two stores in the city and three in the suburbs.

The agreement kept Harold on as director of the museum but removed him from the day-to-day operation of the building. He would conduct tours and schedule exhibits but that was it. A convenience store was set up in the auditorium so those visiting the museum could pick up items like lunch meat or Mama G's chicken pot pie on their way out.

The sign in front of the building was changed to *Big G Grocery and Otis Tharp Fountain Pen Museum*.

The problem was, in their hurry to complete the deal, no one at the *Office Zone* told Harold.

Harold had finished a call from Robert Bidwell, owner of the *Everything Centerline* store who said he was retiring and wondered if Harold was interested in switching to the retail side of the business. He said he would think about it but was just being polite, he wasn't going anywhere as long as the squirrels in the woods behind the museum depended on him.

He heard a commotion in the hallway outside his office and his secretary say, "Sir! You can't..." It was followed by a gruff voice that bellowed, "I'll go where I want," followed by, "you're fired. Pack your things and be out of here by noon or I'll have someone walk you to the door." Then a short, stocky man with the stub of a cigar in his mouth, followed by three men in dark suits, entered his office.

"You can't fire my secretary," Harold said as the man with the cigar walked over to the window and looked out. "She needs the insurance; her husband has serious health issues."

"I'll send a check!" Big G barked and motioned for one of his assistants to take care of it.

"Who are you? What are you doing here?" Harold asked and wondered how he got past Officer Gardner, head of security.

Rather than answer the man grunted, "Dawson."

A young man, Harold guessed was Dawson, stepped forward and said, "He's Big G."

"Big G?" Harold repeated, the name meant nothing to him.

When he saw the confused look on Harold's face he added, "Big G Grocery."

"And he's here because?" Harold couldn't believe a guy who owned a grocery store would walk in his office, throw his weight around, and...

"He owns it."

"A grocery store?" Harold asked, still not following.

"The building. Your office. The whole ball of wax," Dawson said with admiration for what his boss had accomplished.

"There's been a mistake. The building is owned by the *Office Zone*. You can call..."

Dawson pulled a piece of paper from his briefcase, handed it to Harold and said, "Not anymore." Before Harold could read the document, Big G said, "Don't get too comfortable Finebender, you're moving to room 103. This is my office now."

"The security room?" Harold said in surprise. "There's barely enough space for Officer Gardner. He keeps his..."

"There's a small room next to it you can use for whatever it is you do here." After saying it, Big G left. Dawson remained in the doorway and said, "Sorry you had to find out this way. You must feel..." He stopped when Big G hollered, "Keep moving Dawson, he's a big boy, he'll get over it."

Harold was dumbfounded. Before he could read the document Dawson gave him, two men in coveralls entered his office and started putting his things in a cardboard box.

Moving to the security room was a mixed blessing. There were no windows and barely enough room for his desk. The locker Officer Gardner kept his equipment in took up one end of the room. On the other hand, he could see everything going on inside the museum and out because monitors, displaying shots from the security cameras, covered one wall.

The phone rang and when he answered it, Dawson told him, "Big G is holding a meeting in the parking lot and wants you to attend."

"Why?" Harold protested. "I'm not part of..." Dawson hung up before he could finish.

The sky was overcast, the temperature hovered around the freezing mark, and a brisk wind blew across the parking lot, rattling the top of the dumpster. Everyone was bundled up in coats, hats, and scarves except Big G who'd removed his coat and rolled up the sleeves of his blue and white striped shirt.

He pointed in the direction of the woods with the stub of his cigar and asked, "What do you see?"

"A field." "A park." "Trees." The department managers suggested, hoping one of them was right.

When they ran out of ideas, Big G shook his head, disappointed they didn't see what was obvious to him. "I see a stage to showcase our products. A venue for year-round activities." He paused, giving them time to think about what he said. "In the spring we'll hold an Easter egg hunt featuring eggs from free range chickens. In the summer, a barbecue with beef from corn feed cattle. And, for Thanksgiving... a turkey hunt."

"Brilliant." "I can see it." "Great idea Big G." The managers said enthusiastically.

Harold raised a hand. "The woods are owned by the city. You'll need a permit to hold an event there."

"I find it's easier to ask for forgiveness than permission," Big G shot back.

Harold frowned, that didn't sound right to him.

Big G announced, "A few days ago I released a turkey in the woods and, at the end of the week, this place will be crawling with hunters trying to shoot it."

The managers, huddled together, thinking of all that was involved in holding a turkey hunt in the middle of the city.

"Hey!" Big G grunted, "I'm not paying you guys to stand around and shoot the breeze. Get on it!" He tossed the cigar in the dumpster and led them back inside.

After they'd gone, Harold stood at the edge of the parking lot wondering how to let the squirrels know what was coming.

The Big G marketing team met to discuss ways to promote the event. They came up with the slogan, "You tag it and we'll bag it," and made sure the hunters knew that along with the turkey, Big G Grocery would provide all the trimmings for their Thanksgiving meal, including a slow baked, Momma G's sweet potato pie.

The next day brochures showed up in Big G grocery stores letting shoppers know a turkey was loose in the woods behind the fountain pen museum and would go to the first hunter to track it down.

At first the managers thought it would be fun to make them catch the turkey with their bare hands and wondered how many hits they'd get when they posted it on social media. They considered shooting it with paintballs but settled on shotguns. They knew there were restrictions on discharging firearms within city limits, but Big G assured them the company lawyer would tie things up until the event was over.

Billboards around the city advertised the event and the picture of a turkey seen through the cross hairs of a rifle scope, appeared on the side of Big G delivery trucks. Beneath the turkey was the slogan, "You tag it and we'll bag it."

A reporter for the local television station interviewed Toby Gilbert, owner of *Toby's Turkeys*, who'd released the bird in the woods. When asked if he thought a turkey could survive in the wild Toby said, "They're not the smartest creatures in the world but I left a bag of feed for it to eat so it will be okay for a week or two."

The evening before the event, the parking lot was full of campers and pickup trucks. Those wanting to tour the museum had to park on the street, several blocks away. When they finished, hunters followed them to their cars and offered to pay them for their parking place.

Later in the evening RVs rolled in, setting up in the field between the parking lot and the woods. Hunters in camouflage gear slept outside, not wanting the smell of civilization on their clothes. Shots were heard during the night as they made sure their weapons were in working order. The police were called to the museum several times as contestants, forced to stay in the parking lot, argued those in the RVs had an advantage being closer to the woods than they were.

The governor mobilized the Centerline branch of the volunteer guard to patrol the area and dampen tension between contestants. It was a volatile mix, dozens of hunters going after one turkey. Members of an animal rights group joined arms at the edge of the woods and vowed no turkey would be harmed if they had anything to say about it. Several held signs demanding they, "Free the turkey!" And, "Shop, don't shoot."

Big G stood at his office window and chuckled. The turkey hunt cost a bundle, but you don't get advertising like this every day. He saw reporters interviewing hunters and give hourly updates on conditions in the field behind the museum. He considered making it an annual event.

He had no way of knowing the turkey they'd be hunting in the morning, was no longer there.

A few nights before the event, Harold followed his normal routine when leaving for home. He walked to his car, opened the trunk, removed a stack of newspapers, and carried them to the dumpster. When he returned, he closed the trunk and drove out of the parking lot.

That was the way he'd transferred members of the community of squirrels from behind his house to the woods in back of the museum. And it was how he took them to his house if, for some reason, they needed to go there. He didn't check to see if he had passengers. He provided a service, who came and went was none of his business. When he got home, he pulled in the garage and did the same thing in reverse; opened the trunk, walked around like he was looking for something, then closed it, and went upstairs.

He was surprised when, just before hitting the button to close the garage door, he found he was looking at a fully grown turkey standing beside his car, pecking at a tire on his lawn mower.

"What's going on?" his wife Thelma asked when he stepped in the kitchen.

"What do you mean?" he asked innocently.

"You put something in the storage shed. I was standing at the kitchen window and saw you close the door before returning to the garage." After she said it, she put her hands on her hips and tilted her head, challenging him to deny it.

"Oh," Harold said and started for the bedroom to change into more comfortable clothes.

"That's it? That's all you have to say?" She stepped away from the window and asked. "What did Dr. Roberta say about secrets destroying relationships?" After being arrested for reckless driving because she thought there were squirrels in the trunk of her car, she'd been ordered by Judge Muldoon to see a therapist. She found the sessions helpful and encouraged Harold go with her.

Harold raised his hands in an act of surrender. "Okay. You got me. It's a turkey."

She shook her head in disbelief. Of all the things he could have come up with, putting a turkey in the shed would have been the last item on her list. When she saw him walk away from the shed, she thought he'd hidden her Christmas present there. She should have known better, he waited until the last minute to shop. "A turkey?" she said with a laugh. "You come up with the craziest excuses."

Harold had two thoughts. The first was, if she didn't believe him when he told the truth, why bother making things up. The second was. "Stay here, I'll show you."

"No. I believe you. If you say..." she stopped when the garage door opened, and she watched him jog across the yard. He opened the door of the shed, went inside, and came out leading a turkey with a leash made from a piece of clothesline. When he saw her at the window, he smiled and pointed at the turkey, pecking at a bug in the grass. He looked to see what kind of bug it was and, when he turned to get her reaction, she'd gone.

The morning after the turkey hunt, Harold opened the newspaper and read the headline, "BIG G GROCERY SUED FOR FALSE ADVERTISING!" Monty Bison, a prominent lawyer in Centerline and a big game hunter told a reporter, "Look, I've tracked animals all over the world and can tell you for a fact there's no turkey in those woods. They may have run one through for a photo op, but that's it."

Other hunters quoted in the article repeated Monty's complaint and said they were joining him in a class action lawsuit, suing Big G for what he'd done.

Harold couldn't help smiling at the knowledge that the turkey that showed up in his garage, was back with its buddies at *Toby's Turkeys*. He hadn't thought much about how it got in the trunk of his car but was pretty sure the squirrels in the woods had something to do with it.

He was rinsing a bowl before putting it in the dishwasher when the doorbell rang. "Would you get that sweetheart I'm running a little late." His question was met with the sound of the shower in the bathroom turning on. He opened the door and found Myron Boggs, standing on the front step, facing the street. At the sound of the door opening, Myron spun around and demanded, "Where is it?"

"I'm sorry?" Harold stammered.

"The turkey. Where'd you put it?" He looked behind Harold thinking he was keeping it in the house as a pet. "I received a complaint and as president of the Sunny Hill Estates Homeowners Association, I am obligated to investigate."

"Someone said they saw a..."

Myron nodded. "Yesterday afternoon you were seen in your backyard with a turkey. Article 27b of the homeowner's agreement prohibits housing, boarding, or keeping poultry on your property." He shoved a copy of the agreement toward him with the part about no poultry highlighted and underlined.

"I don't know what you're talking about Myron." Harold said innocently. "Whoever said it must have..."

"It's payback, isn't it?" Myron said and shook his head in disappointment.

"Payback?" Harold repeated, caught off guard by the comment.

"There was a lot going on in my life last year. I was desperate. Everyone at *Marina Del Aqua* was reeling in new members fore and aft and I hadn't a nibble. As commodore of the fleet, I should have been setting the example, landing the big fish."

Harold interrupted. "What's that got to do with me?"

Myron waved his hands. "We've gone off course, sailed into shallow water. This is about you and a turkey."

"Go ahead, look around," Harold said, realizing nothing would be gained by arguing with him.

"I did."

"And?"

"The door to your shed is locked but I heard something moving inside."

"Something moving in the shed?" Harold asked, surprised by the comment.

Myron leaned toward him and said, "It's show time Harold." He owns several video and game rental stores and tends to talk in theatrical terms. "The stage is set so what do you say we dim the lights and raise the curtain."

"I'll meet you at the garage but make it quick, I have to get to work. I'm expecting an important phone call," Harold said as he closed the door, picked up his briefcase, hollered goodbye to Thelma, and went down the stairs to the garage. When the door opened, Myron was waiting for him in the driveway with a book of code violation slips in his hand.

When they reached the shed Harold unlocked the door and opened it. Myron stepped inside and looked around. Harold was glad after Toby left with the turkey, he'd taken time to clean the shed. There was nothing to suggest one had been there.

Myron flipped his fingers a gesture Harold took to mean he could close the door. "The comment about the yacht club..."

"Is forgotten," Harold said as they walked back to the garage. Before getting in his car he asked, "Are we done here?"

Myron nodded. He wished he knew Harold better. If he did, he would have mentioned Sylvia, his wife of thirty-three years, had moved out. She said she needed space to breath and time to find her bliss. With networks streaming movies to smart phones and electronic tablets, video rental sales had dried up. He was barely making ends meet the way it was, a messy divorce would wipe out his meager savings and put his membership at the yacht club in danger of being revoked.

He didn't respond when Harold honked as he backed out of the garage and drove to the street.

When Harold got to the museum, he tapped the code on the keypad outside the security room, opened the door, and was hit with the smell of a wet tobacco. He stepped inside and saw Big G standing in front of one of the monitors. "A little further," he told Officer Gardner who moved the mouse to advance the film.

"There!" Big G shouted, turned to Harold and growled, "I knew you'd be trouble the moment we met. I should never have agreed to let you stay."

Harold looked around, not sure who he was talking to, the room was filled with managers from Big G grocery stores.

"I'm talking to you Finebender. You're twisting in the wind, hanging by a thread. It went against my instincts to keep you around and, to show your gratitude, you pull something like this. That's the thanks I get for being a nice guy" He pointed to the screen in front of him.

"I just got..." before he could say here, Big G told Officer Gardner to, "Roll it," and waved for Harold to come over and stand next to him.

On the monitor, Harold saw himself leave the building, stopping to make sure the door closed behind him. He continued across the parking lot at a leisurely pace, glancing at the sky, wondering if he'd make it home before it rained. He got in his car then smacked his forehead like he forgot something. He got out, opened the trunk, removed a bundle of newspapers, and carried them to the dumpster.

"There it is!" Big G shouted, pointing at the screen. While Harold was at the dumpster, his car lurched forward, then settled back to its original position. As the video continued, Harold closed the trunk, got in and drove away.

Big G shook his head and asked, "Do I look like I fell off a turnip truck?"

Harold didn't know what to say because he didn't understand the question. "I carried newspapers to the dumpster. I usually do it when I arrive for work, but I was..."

"Save it for someone who cares," Big G said angrily before asking, "What flew in the trunk?"

"Flew in..."

"The blur. The object. Something." Big G growled. "It looked like a turkey, traveling at a high rate of speed."

"A turkey? In my trunk?" Harold chuckled. "I don't think so."

"Well, I do," Big G shot back. "When a guy takes something out of the trunk, he closes it before walking away. You didn't."

"My hands were full," Harold protested.

"Use an elbow. A foot. Whatever." It took Harold a moment to realize Big G was stalling for time. He wondered why until he glanced at the monitor and saw a panel truck with *The Lock Doc* on the side of his truck park behind his car. A tall, thin man in white coveralls got out, shoved a tool near the lock on the trunk and popped it open. He looked inside, then turned toward the camera on the back of the building and raised his hands, letting Big G know he saw nothing to suggest a turkey had been there.

"This isn't over," Big G growled, threw his cigar in the wastebasket, swore he'd get to the bottom of this if it was the last thing he did, and stomped out of the room. The managers hurried after him saying, "I saw it Big G." "The car definitely moved." "Did Doctor Lock look behind the spare tire?"

When he was sure Big G wasn't coming back, Officer Gardner closed the door, returned to the keyboard, and said solemnly, "There's something you should see." He tapped a few keys, moved the mouse over an icon, and pressed the button. The monitor flickered and

Harold found he was looking at his car, parked where it was when Big G was watching the video.

He started say he'd seen it when Big G was here when an object the size of a pillow flew over his car and landed in the parking lot. He watched in disbelief as half a dozen squirrels ran by his car, picked the object up, and ran out of camera range.

A few minutes later the object reappeared, this time landing on the hood of his car. The team of squirrels retrieved it. Officer Gardner advanced the video and said, "That happened a number of times until," he hit the enter key, the film slowed to normal speed, and Harold saw the object hit the trunk of his car and fall to the ground.

"They did it a few more times to make sure the first one wasn't a fluke." Officer Gardner said like he couldn't believe he was talking about this.

"Did you show this to Big G?" Harold asked, sure if he had, his days at the museum were over.

Officer Gardner shook his head, "What he doesn't know won't hurt him. He was here when I arrived for work, that's how I got roped into doing his dirty work."

Harold laughed and said, "So that's how they did it." He was sure if he lifted the object, they used to get the distance right, it would weigh the same as the turkey he found in his garage.

He was glad Big G hadn't asked why he'd hesitated before closing the trunk lid. That's the problem with guys like him Harold thought, once they come up with an answer, there not open to new information.

DRONE ON

Lloyd Brewster was a typical kid growing up in a suburb of Centerline, good at some things, not so good at others. He dreamed of becoming a major league baseball player, but it was obvious at an early age that wasn't going to happen. While at bat he had trouble following the ball when it left the pitcher's hand. If he managed to get a hit, he was so slow running to first base Coach Berm would holler, "Take it around the horn boys." The third baseman would scoop up the ball, throw it to the other infielders, then toss it to first before Lloyd got there.

With no athletic skills to pave the way to a promising future, his fate was sealed. He would join the family business, doing odd jobs around town, counting the days until retirement.

All that changed when he took a required science class his first semester at middle school. It didn't happen overnight; it was a gradual process. When he got his first report card, he received average grades in other subjects but got outstanding in *Introduction to Scientific Thought*. It was like someone flipped a switch and a light came on.

To earn money to buy equipment to do experiments at home, he took a part time job at the Big G Grocery in his neighborhood, delivering groceries on his bicycle.

While other boys his age studied the sports section of the newspaper, Lloyd read articles on science and technology, eager to discover the latest breakthrough. His parents ate supper before he got home because they couldn't take another meal listening to some theory about the effect of sunspots on mobile phone reception. Or hear something Ms. Fletcher, his physics teacher, said in class that day.

Because he'd neglected other subjects in his single-minded pursuit of science, his grade point average wasn't good enough to earn a scholarship to attend college. So, after graduating from high school, he went to work full time at Big G Grocery.

When his father retired, his parents moved to a fifty-five and older community in Florida, but Lloyd stayed behind. He asked the manager of the store if he could turn the storage room above the loading dock into an apartment.

When the door to college closed, the one to the world of science opened. Soon his small apartment was filled with instruction manuals, high fidelity speakers, and a high-speed computer with dual monitors.

The manager, aware of Lloyd's interest in technology, put him to work fixing problems around the store when he wasn't delivering groceries. He no longer had to wait for a repairman, losing products by the second when a cooler shutdown, Lloyd was there to get it up and running. When a software glitch prevented the cash registers from keeping track of customer preferences, Lloyd had the system back online in minutes. On and on, problems that occur every day in the grocery business, were taken care of by the youngest employee at the store, working for a minimum wage.

His manager tried to increase his salary, but Big G turned down the request, as far as he was concerned, delivery boys were a dime a dozen. The manager got around it by not charging him for the apartment,

His scientific interests went in a new direction when, during a lunch break, he read an article in a magazine about the growing use of drones by large companies to inspect leaks in oil lines or loose connections on telephone poles. Before long, customers using the Big G pharmacy, found their prescriptions waiting on their front porch when they got home, delivered by a drone with the Big G logo on the side, piloted skillfully by Lloyd Brewster.

His reputation as a prodigy grew but Lloyd couldn't care less. Work at the store, menial as it was, gave him time and a little money to pursue his passion; science and everything related to it.

Roscoe heard it before he saw it. A high-pitched hum in the distance, growing louder as it got closer. He closed his eyes and tried to remember the picture Sparky, the community technical genius, showed him in the catalog. He removed the small piece of black tape he'd stuck to the edge of his nest and waited. The craft making the noise got closer and soon was hovering outside his nest. He counted to three then reached out and stuck the tape on the place where Sparky said the camera for the guidance system was located. The plane spun out of control, slamming into the trunk of his tree as it fell to the ground. He climbed out of his nest, anxious to get a closer look. He heard a motor grinding inside the plane and guessed the guidance system was trying to get the craft airborne. He waited for Marvin and Jules to help carry the damaged plane to Sparky's lab.

Lloyd couldn't figure out what went wrong. Things were working perfectly until the screen on his laptop turned blue. He inspected the line connecting the computer to the Internet. Everything checked out, which meant something happened to the plane when it entered the woods.

He followed the signals from the drones GPS to the woods behind the *Big G Grocery and Otis Tharp Fountain Pen Museum.* As he walked along, he had the feeling he was being watched but when he turned to look, no one was there.

The GPS in the drone emitted a series of short beeps so it didn't take long for him to find it at the base of a tree set apart from others. An examination of the plane showed it hadn't suffered serious damage. A closer look revealed tool marks on the propeller, like someone had straightened it. He looked for a house nearby where a person with the skill and the proper equipment could perform the precision work required to repair the blade lived. He wondered why someone would straighten the propeller and leave the plane in the woods? Why not contact him? There were enough identifying marks on the wings to figure out who it belonged to. They couldn't miss the Big G logo on the wings.

He almost dropped the plane when the propeller started spinning. It didn't make sense; the joystick and computer program required to start the plane and control its flight were in his room above the loading dock. The drone left his hand, flew around the open space, and made a perfect landing. The propeller stopped turning as it taxied across the ground and stopped when it bumped into the toe of his shoe.

He shook his head, trying to make sense of it. The guidance system on the drone would only work with the software on his laptop. A password and a series of detailed instructions describing the flight plan were required before taking off.

Yet it flew.

Something strange was going on. He decided to go to his apartment, get the miniature camera he kept on his workbench, mount it in a tree, and aim it where he found the plane. He was about to leave when, on a whim, he picked up a stick and drew a grid with nine boxes in the dirt. He found a stone and placed it in the top box on the left side. He'd find out if the person who fixed the propeller was up for a game of tic-tac-toe.

It took a while for him to find the camera. Like most creative people, neatness and organization were not high on his list of priorities. The manager bought it when things were being taken from the fruit baskets on the sidewalk in front of the store. Lloyd was able to catch the thief in action using the camera linked to his computer. When the manager learned the culprit was a homeless veteran, he refused to press chargers. The next time the veteran walked by the manager stopped him and explained the fruit that didn't sell that day was put in a bin in back of the store. If someone didn't take it, it went to the landfill with the rest of the garbage.

Occasionally the veteran found a loaf of day-old bread or a box of cereal past its sell by date in the bin with the fruit.

Lloyd didn't know how long it would take for the person who repaired the drones propeller to return, so he replaced the batteries in the camera with new ones, and checked to made sure it was communicating with his laptop. As an afterthought, he taped a note with his name and how to contact him on the back in case someone found it and wondered what a camera was doing in a tree in the middle of the woods. When he was sure everything was working properly, he left his apartment and headed for the woods. He felt he was on a fool's errand, sure whoever repaired the plane was long gone and all he would see were falling leaves and wildlife walking by.

After placing the camera in the tree and checking his laptop to make sure it was aimed where he wanted, he climbed down. As he walked past the place where he found the drone, he looked at the ground and saw a stick in the middle box of the grid he'd drawn. Someone was messing with him, there was no doubt about it. He'd find out who it was when they showed up on his computer screen. He studied the grid, placed a stone in the box below the one he put there before and left, anxious to get home and start the surveillance.

He went straight to his workbench, not stopping to change clothes, dirty from climbing the tree and walking in the woods. He wanted to make sure the signal from the camera was strong enough to reach his apartment. As the scene on the monitor slowly came into focus, he saw two squirrels standing beside the grid he'd drawn. One started to leave but the one with him grabbed his arm, pointed at the camera he'd placed in the tree, and the screen went blank.

Lloyd rebooted his computer and logged back in, but nothing changed. He unplugged it from the power strip, waited a few seconds, then plugged it back in.

He didn't understand what went wrong, it was working perfectly then stopped.

He was about to go back to the woods, thinking there was a problem with the camera when the monitor flickered, and he found he was looking at the face of a squirrel. The squirrel shook his head, moved a paw toward the camera, and the screen on his laptop went dark. Lloyd sat back, dumbfounded. Although it went against everything he knew about animal behavior, the squirrel had not only located the camera but figured out how to turn it on and off.

The field between the fountain pen museum and the woods has been used for a number of things over the years. A walking trail, a soccer field, and dog park to name a few. Each lasted a while then was abandoned as people's interests changed. The dog park proved to be a disaster as, once off their leash, the animals either caught the scent of a racoon and ran into the woods, picking up cockle burrs and ticks or dashed across the parking lot and into the street frightening pedestrians and causing traffic jams.

Recently it was used for a turkey hunt that ended in disaster with hunters suing Big G Grocery for false advertising.

The field was currently occupied by three boys playing catch. When the ball sailed over the head of one of the boys and bounced in the woods, he stopped chasing it and looked at the other two for help.

"I double dog dare you to put a foot in the woods," the chubby boy with the burr haircut shouted. The second boy said something the third boy couldn't hear but guessed he'd repeated the dare. He'd heard stories about what happens to boys who go in the woods alone. But it was a double dog dare and all he had to do was step over the boundary where the field stopped, and the trees began. When he did, they'd get off his back about not catching the ball as well as they did.

He stuck a foot in the woods and quickly brought it back. The other two laughed, called him a chicken, and said it didn't count unless both feet crossed the line.

He did and to prove he was up to the challenge, took another step.

"Last one in the woods is a dork," the one with the burr haircut shouted as he ran past him and was soon lost among the tree trunks and bushes that grew to enormous size because the lawn service was only responsible for mowing the field, their work stopped at the edge of the woods.

The second boy eagerly followed.

The third boy heard them laughing and shouting as they ran through the woods, pulling up weeds with clods of dirt on the end, and throwing them at each other.

The moment the boys entered the woods, a signal spread through the squirrel community telling its members to go to their safe place and stay there until the all clear was given. Some ran to the meeting room, others hunkered down in their nests.

Ignoring the warning, Sparky left his lab and climbed the tree where the camera was located. He planned to record the event and show members of *Young Squirrels in Action* what happens when small humans are in the woods.

When the boys entered the area the one with the burr haircut brought a finger to his lips, telling his friend to be quiet then pointed at the squirrel in the tree. With as little movement as possible, they felt on the ground for a rock or clod of dirt large enough o throw. The leader silently counted down and when he reached zero shouted, "Bombs away!" His rock missed the target but the one from his friend connected, knocking Sparky to the ground where he landed awkwardly and lay motionless.

Lloyd ate lunch in his apartment because the breakroom was too noisy for him to concentrate on what he was reading. The manager knew where to find him if a problem came up before his lunch hour was over. So, he climbed the stairs to his apartment planning to fiddle with the software he'd recently installed on his computer.

He'd unwrapped the sandwich, placed it on a paper plate, and opened a soft drink when he heard a series of high-pitched beeps coming from his laptop, letting him know someone had turned on the camera he left in the woods. Curious, he glanced at the screen and saw a squirrel on the ground, an arm bent in an unnatural position. As it lay there, he saw two boys pick sticks to finish off their helpless victim.

There wasn't enough time for him to go to the woods on his bicycle before the boys finished off the injured squirrel. Calling the museum was out, he'd have to go through who knows how many employees to reach someone willing to do something, by then it would be too late. He was sure calling 911 to report a squirrel was in danger, would bring a stern warning and a reminder not to tie up the phone with frivolous reports.

He glanced at the shelves that held his equipment, searching for an answer. Between his wireless headphones and a laptop, he was repairing for a friend, was the drone he'd flown to the woods a week earlier. He opened the window in his apartment, fired up the motor, and turned it loose.

He ran to his computer, and with a few keystrokes, turned on the built-in guidance system. Since he hadn't flown it recently it was still programmed to go to the woods. Sailing over traffic on the street and skillfully avoiding telephone poles, the drone flew over the museum parking lot and the field behind it.

The boy who'd failed to catch the ball, looked up when he heard the buzz of the plane's motor as it sailed over his head and entered the woods. He stood with his mouth open as it dodged tree trunks and ducked under low hanging branches.

Then it was out of sight.

They two boys cautiously approached the creature on the ground. They'd been warned about the danger of being bitten by disease carrying animals, so they poked it for signs of life. Finding none, they moved closer to the wounded creature, raised their sticks, and were about to deliver the finishing blow when they heard a buzz, and saw an airplane hovering a few feet above their heads. It remained motionless as a built-in camera took their picture. The boy with the burr haircut swung his stick, barely missing the airplane. Or it moved, it was hard to tell. As it dodged additional blows, it slowly moved away from the fallen creature. The other boy crept behind the plane, swung his stick, and clipped a wing. It tilted to one side then righted itself.

The first boy, encouraged by the success of his friend screamed as he ran toward the plane, flailing away. He had no luck, but his partner did, landing a solid blow that knocked off the damaged wing, sending the plane spiraling to the ground.

The boys stomped and kicked it until there wasn't enough left to suggest it was nothing but an odd collection of airplane parts.

They looked at each other, crouched, then jumped forward and shouted, "Booyah," as they bumped chests in victory. They'd defeated the advanced guard, now it was time to finish what they were doing before the plane arrived. They turned, raised their sticks, and discovered the injured squirrel was gone.

It didn't make sense. It was on the ground, out cold from being struck by a rock and injured by the fall. They poked the bushes with their sticks but didn't find it.

With the victim gone and nothing left to destroy, they decided it was time to go. They followed the path they took to get there but after walking a few minutes, found they were deeper in the woods than when they started. They were sure they turned at the flowering shrub on the left side of the path. They backtracked, looking for footprints or scuff marks they'd made on the way in.

While trying to figure out which way to go, they were bombarded by walnuts and acorns thrown by squirrels on the tree limbs above them. They screamed, ran down a path, tripped over an exposed root, and rolled in a patch of poison ivy. They leapt up, plunged through the tall grass, and shouted with relief when they saw the field and the museum beyond.

As they staggered out of the woods, they were met by Lloyd Brewster and a man in a police uniform. The boy with the burr haircut started crying and begged them not to tell his parents he went in the woods. He looked for the third boy but guessed he took off when they entered the woods, every fear he had of dark places overcoming his concern for his friends.

Officer Gardner didn't have the authority to arrest anyone. He wore a uniform and carried a gun but only for show, he had no bullets to put in it. Besides, the boys hadn't broken any laws. There were no, *Do Not Enter* signs posted at the edge of the woods. There were laws about the abusing animals but without an eyewitness, there wasn't enough evidence to bring charges against them.

"Get out of here," Officer Gardner said in a gruff voice. "I don't want to see you two around here again. You hear me?"

The boys mumbled, "Yes sir," and took off for the parking lot where they left their bicycles.

After thanking the officer for his help, Lloyd entered the woods and followed the path he took when he put the camera in the tree. When he reached the open space, he looked for the injured squirrel but couldn't find it. He heard a noise behind him and when he turned to see what it was, a group of squirrels left the safety of the tall grass and stepped into the open space. They looked at each other then held up a sign with, "Think U," on it. By the time he figured out what it said, they were gone, vanishing as quickly as they appeared.

One remained by the trunk of a tree. He had a bandage around his head, and an arm in a sling. He pointed, letting Lloyd know where the camera was located, opened a door in the base of the tree, and stepped inside.

Lloyd gathered the pieces of the drone he thought he could use and was about to leave when he glanced at the grid he'd drawn. Starting at the box on the lower left and going at an angle to the top box on the right, a row of sticks formed a line, winning the game.

On his way to his apartment, he stopped by the library near the grocery store to see if they had any books on animal intelligence, specifically members of the squirrel family.

A SQUIRREL AND A HUMAN WALK IN A MUSEUM

Roscoe walked to the edge of the woods where Norman was standing guard. He had the dusk to midnight watch, looking for signs of activity around Seed Man's building. The reason he was there, the reason for the whole *keep an eye on the building* schedule, was because Seed Man hadn't been seen in two days. His car was parked by the dumpster but hadn't moved since leaving it there.

At a meeting of the *Committee for the Protection of Neighborhood Resources* someone mentioned they'd waited by the dumpster, ready to jump in the trunk of his car for a ride back to their previous home behind his house but he hadn't shown up. They called it *Riding With Seed Man*. When he got home, he opened the trunk and acted like he was looking for something in the garage, giving his passengers time to get out before closing the garage door, turning off the lights, going and upstairs.

The next morning the process was reversed and the community member, his business completed, rode back to the woods.

Roscoe's agenda for the meeting was shoved aside when Lothar, a new member of the committee, asked if anyone had seen Seed Man, his car hadn't moved in days. He produced a paper with names in boxes, breaking the day into units and assigning someone to watch his building 24/7. He made a motion that the committee approve his plan and, after looking at the list and not seeing their names on it, they approved his plan unanimously.

Roscoe was amazed at how quickly it was approved. A request for a new shelf in the library took at least two meetings and a trip there to make sure it was needed. Eventually they'd turn the problem over to the library committee to decide what to do about it.

"See anything?" Roscoe asked.

Norman shook his head and grumbled, "No Seed Man. No activity. No nothing." He took a deep breath and let it out before asking, "Can I go home? This is boring."

Roscoe would like to have said yes, he didn't know what all the fuss was about, Seed Man could come and go as he pleased. But the committee voted to post a guard and until they abandoned the program, his paws were tied. "Let's take a walk," he said and started across the field toward Seed Man's building.

"I don't think... I mean, I'm not supposed to..." The last thing Norman wanted was to get caught away from his post. He'd heard rumors Lothar showed up unexpectedly to catch whoever was on duty asleep or goofing around with friends, the fate of the community forgotten.

"It's okay, you're with me," Roscoe said and waited for Norman to decide if he was on the level or if this was a trick to see if he'd leave his post. He knew if he did, Lothar would be on him like seeds in a feeder.

As they approached the front of the building, Roscoe noticed the light above the entrance was off. He looked through the window next to the door and saw it was dark inside. He was about to leave, guessing it was late and the building was closed for the day when he noticed the door wasn't completely closed. Curious, he pushed it with his foot and was surprised when it opened an inch or two.

He was wondering if he should close the door or leave it like it was, when he was hit with the beam of a flashlight, heard footsteps on the sidewalk, and someone shout, "We gets im." He had no idea what it meant, he hadn't taken the *Human Sounds and What They Mean* class in seed school, but didn't need to, to know he was in trouble.

He shouted for Norman to run but was too late, he took off when he saw the door to the building was open. The two humans walked up the steps with their arms out to stop him if he tried to go around them.

He wished he'd left when Norman did. Now, with his escape route blocked, he was left with one option. He squeezed through the open door, closed it behind him and breathed a sigh of relief when he heard a click as it locked. He stood in the dark hall, listening to the humans, pound on the door and shout for him to, "Opening the doorski."

Eventually the shouting stopped, and he realized since Seed Man brought them to the woods, this was the first time he'd been in his building.

(Earlier that day.)

Harold Finebender waited for traffic to clear before turning into the parking lot of the *Big G Grocery and Otis Tharp Fountain Pen Museum*. He drove to his reserved parking place, backed in, and turned off the motor. He got out and, like he'd done dozens of times before, opened the trunk, removed a bundle of newspapers, and carried it to the dumpster.

He wanted to allow time for his passengers, if he had any, to get out, so he picked up scraps of paper that escaped when the cleaning crew emptied the trash. When enough time passed, he closed the trunk, and walked to the backdoor of the museum.

He entered his office, saw Officer Gardner, asked how things went during the night and got the usual, "Same old same old."

He went to Penultimate, the coffee shop on the second floor, and was disappointed to find his favorite blend, *Night in Madagascar* had been replaced by the *Mama G's 50-50, half caf half decaf.*

He was on the way to his office when he saw a man sitting at the table in the conference area outside the security room. He explained who he was and asked if he could help. The man introduced himself as Rheingold Given, former Ambassador to Galvonia. He explained it was former because the nation of Galvonia no longer existed, it had been swallowed up by Gludistan, its neighbor.

None of what he said made sense to Harold. He'd traveled abroad a few times representing the museum at fountain pen conferences but not to the countries the ambassador mentioned.

With the introductions out of the way and after sending his aide for coffee, the ambassador got down to business. "What I am about to tell you must not leave the room. Is that understood?"

Harold nodded.

"After lengthy discussions to avoid a civil war, a document was signed that committed both countries to negotiate in good faith. Neither would cause trouble for the other and the people of Galvonia would go on with their lives without fear of being attacked" He reached in his briefcase, removed a box, and wondered if it was wise to drag Harold into the danger in store for the one who possessed what was inside. Deciding he'd come this far, and the museum was the perfect place to display it he said, "I have the pen used to sign the agreement."

He placed the box on the table, removed the lid, and took out what looked to Harold like a cheap ball point pen, the kind you could buy in a pack of ten at an office supply store for a couple of dollars. The top that covered the ball point was missing and it looked like the owner had chewed on the part that remained.

When he saw the puzzled look on Harold's face the ambassador explained. "We were in a hurry, it belonged to a reporter covering the event." He leaned toward Harold and said in a serious tone, "Not everyone in Galvonia is happy with the agreement. Those who oppose it will go to great lengths to destroy the instrument they see as a symbol of a government that sold them out and destroyed the country they love."

Harold was about to ask if there wasn't a better place to keep the pen, like the embassy, or a government office when the ambassador's aide rushed in and said loud enough for Harold to hear, "They've found us Mr. Ambassador, we have to leave immediately."

The ambassador stood, turned to Harold, and asked, "Do you have a car?"

Harold nodded, pulled the keys from his pocket, and told him where he was parked.

"Your car will be returned when the ambassador is safe," the aide said as he put the pen back in the box and hurried out the door to the parking lot.

Moments after the ambassador left, someone forced the door to the museum open, and two men with heavily accented voices entered. Harold guessed the Galvonians the ambassador mentioned, had come for the pen. He looked for a place to hide it, spotted a cup full of pens on Officer Gardner's desk, and stuck it in the middle of them. He tossed the box in the waste basket and was about to push it under the desk with his foot when the door to his office was forced open. and two burly looking men wearing a uniform of some kind, entered. One stood by the door, keeping an eye on the hallway, the other walked over to Harold and said, "Whirs et?"

"Et?" Harold asked and would have moved away from Officer Gardner's desk, but the intruder was so close he couldn't get by him without looking like he was hiding something.

"De penski," the intruder grunted.

"Penski?" Harold was lost, nothing the man said made sense.

The visitor pointed to the cup of pens on Officer Gardner's desk, and said slowly, "De pen ski."

Harold raised his hands, letting him know he didn't understand.

The intruder glanced at the waste basket and saw the box Harold threw there. The bottom made it in but the top didn't. He picked it up, looked Harold in the eye and growled, "Use am sum kine of jokingster?"

Harold shrugged.

The man held the box inches from Harold's face and growled, "Fur las tim, whir es de penski?"

Harold had hoped to stall long enough for Officer Gardner to finish his rounds and make it back to the security room. When he didn't show up, he decided to try a different approach.

"Oh," he said and nodded like he'd just figured out what the intruder was talking about. "The penski is in," he pointed to the ceiling, "the International Pens Room on the second floor."

The man turned to the one at the door and said something Harold didn't understand. His partner pointed to where he was standing and said, "Flour de onesk." He pointed to the ceiling, "Flour de twosk." After a nod the first one grabbed Harold's arm, pulled him out of the room and said, "Taking us to flour de twosk."

On the way to the stairs, Harold saw Officer Gardner tied to a chair and blindfolded. "This is not good," he groaned as he put a foot on the first step.

Midge was new to the Community of Abner; a friend invited her to stay with her until she could afford a nest of her own. She'd heard about the riding with Seed Man arrangement but hadn't caught all the details. She remembered her friend saying the trunk was open for a short time, so you had to get in before it closed. She had no idea what a trunk was.

That's why she was hanging around the dumpster while others in the community were at the feeder or on their way to work. She was trying to think of something to do while she waited when the door to Seed Man's building opened, and two humans hurried across the parking lot. She'd only heard of Seed Man, she hadn't seen him, so she guessed he was one of those approaching the car.

She picked up the bundle of items she'd brought with her and leaned forward, ready to move the moment the trunk opened.

The ambassador's aide pressed the place on the key that unlocked the doors and slid in the front seat. The ambassador joined him on the passenger side. They were so busy looking for angry Galvonians, they didn't notice Midge leap in the car moments before the ambassador closed the door. Safely inside, she crouched on the floor behind the driver's seat.

The car tore out of the parking lot, leaving tracks of rubber on the asphalt, and cut in front of a city bus as it shot across the street. The bus driver slammed on the brakes and leaned on the horn. The ambassador looked in the rearview mirror and saw a man in a camouflage outfit, run down the steps in front of the museum to see what caused the commotion.

Midge clung to the carpet as the car slid around corners, skidded to a stop, then accelerated when the traffic light changed. She heard voices in front of her but had no idea what they were saying. Soon the car stopped, the engine turned off, and the doors opened. It happened so fast it took her by surprise. She reached for the bundle she brought with her and discovered it had slid under the seat she was hiding behind during the hectic ride. By the time she found it, the doors closed, trapping her inside.

She climbed up the seat, expecting to see Seed Man's yard and the shed her friend said served as the temporary meeting room for the squirrels who'd stayed behind when the others left. Instead, she saw buildings with broken windows, trash in the street, and clumps of grass growing between cracks in the sidewalk.

She guessed she fell asleep because her first sensation was of movement. Not at the breakneck speed like before, but slowly and deliberately. She clung to the bundle with both paws, determined to be ready the next time the door opened. When it did, she leaped out, and found she was standing by the dumpster where she'd been waiting earlier.

As the human walked away, she started across the field, anxious to get to her friend's place convinced the riding with Seed Man thing was a joke the community played on newcomers like her. She didn't slow down when Sheldon, on duty for the daylight to noon watch hollered, "Halt. Who goes there?"

Midge continued walking and when challenged a second time, spun around, put her paws on her hips, looked Sheldon in the eye and said, "Who goes there is the best you got?"

Sheldon watched her walk away and decided he wouldn't stop her no matter what Lothar said.

(Back to the present.)

Roscoe waited for his eyes to adjust to the darkness in the hallway before moving. When they did, he walked down the wide aisle, listening for a sound to break the deadly silence. He jumped when something crashed on the floor above him. It was followed by angry voices, and it didn't take someone skilled in interpreting human sounds to understand the human talking was upset he hadn't found what he was looking for.

He saw a human tied to a chair and was going to help him when the tone of the voices on the floor above him changed, and two humans forced Seed Man to the top of the stairs. Roscoe was totally exposed and thought the mood the men with Seed Man were in might be lightened by taking a pot shot at a defenseless creature. The only thing he saw he thought could help was a red, rectangular box halfway up the wall. There was no way he could jump that high, so he looked for something he could use to reach it.

There was the chair the human was in, but knew he couldn't budge it. He saw a bucket and mop in a corner and guessed a worker had been cleaning the floor and fled when the intruders entered the building. He saw the feet and legs of the men descend the stairs and knew he was running out of time. He raced across the floor, leapt over the bucket, and grabbed the mop handle. He climbed to the top, pressed his feet against the wall and pushed. The handle stalled when it was sticking straight up so he shifted his weight from one side to the other and it continued toward the wall.

"What's im doinsk?" one of the men shouted as he ran down the stairs.

Roscoe focused on the red object on the wall and when he got close, let go of the mop handle, grabbed the lever, and hung on for dear life. He felt it drop down but was disappointed when nothing happened.

He was a sitting duck, a gray shape on a white wall, clinging to a handle attached to a red box. He heard an alarm start slowly then grow to an earsplitting wail. Emergency lights flashed on and off. The intruders looked at each other, not sure what was going on.

The sprinklers turned on, covering everything with a thick, gooey foam.

Roscoe let go of the handle, dropped to the ground and ran across the slippery floor. He'd reached the entrance when the door opened and humans in odd looking outfits rushed in, pulling a hose behind them.

When the last human entered the museum, Roscoe hurried out before the door closed, ran across the lawn, and hid behind the sign directing visitors to the parking lot. He waited until Seed Man, with a blanket over his shoulders, stepped outside. "No," he explained to the one helping him, "I have no idea what set off the alarm."

Officer Gardner came out next, shaking his arms to get circulation back after being tied up for so long. The blindfold that had covered his eyes, hung loosely around his neck.

Two humans, Roscoe recognized as the men on the stairs, were taken to a police car and helped inside. When he was sure Seed Man was safe, he crossed the field, anxious to go to his nest and let Penny Sue, his life partner, know he was okay. He reached the entrance to the woods when Sheldon stepped from behind a tree and demanded he stop and identify himself.

Roscoe shook his head and told him, "Not today, Sheldon. Not after what I've been through."

As he watched him enter the woods, Sheldon wondered what good he was doing if no one stopped when he told them to.

When the cleanup was complete and employees allowed back in the building, Harold found Office Gardner in the security room, standing in front of the wall of monitors. When he saw Harold, he told him the security system was back online. "The intruders turned off the power to the cameras so there's no record of them being here." He shook his head and mumbled, "They didn't look that smart to me."

Harold started toward his desk but stopped when Officer Gardner said, "Something's bothered me about the alarm going off. I can't stop thinking about it."

Harold waited.

Officer Gardner shook his head like he was trying to dislodge a bad memory. "The two goons jumped me when I came out of the *Historical Pens of Centerline Room,* tied me to a chair, and blindfolded me." He shuddered at the memory but shook it off, hoping telling Harold what he saw would provide closure to a terrible experience.

"I fell asleep while sitting there. The siren woke me. It took some work, but I managed to pull a corner of the blindfold down far enough to see what was going on." He hesitated, not sure Harold would believe what he was about to say. "This is going to sound crazy but before the sprinklers turned on, I saw," this was the hard part, but he'd come this far so there was no turning back, "a squirrel."

Harold raised an eyebrow when he mentioned a squirrel.

"It was hanging from the fire alarm." Officer Gardner lifted his hands like he wished the story had a different ending, but it was what it was. "The sprinklers came on and when the fire department arrived, the squirrel was gone."

Harold smiled. What he said didn't sound crazy to him, it made perfect sense.

BUM RAP

"I'm sorry, I didn't catch your name?" Roscoe was listening but missed it.

"Snowy Winters," the person across from him said as he shuffled through papers in his briefcase.

"Is that a family name or..." before Roscoe could finish the stranger said, "It was my stage name when I was performing." He leaned forward and spoke so quietly Roscoe had trouble hearing him say, "Rex. My name is Rex."

"And you're here because?" When he entered the meeting room, Roscoe glanced at the calendar on the wall behind his secretary's desk and saw nothing scheduled until the afternoon. He was hoping to use the time to catch up on paperwork, as usual he was hopelessly behind.

"I'm the booking agent for the hottest property in show business today. SRO wherever he performs. Ticket sales through the roof. Lines at theaters backed up for blocks." Rex sat back and smiled like he was about to give Roscoe a valuable gift.

"SRO?" Roscoe asked, not familiar with the term.

"Standing Room Only," Rex said proudly.

"And you think...?"

"I don't think Mr. Chairman, I know. This is an opportunity to put your community on the map. To say to other communities, get on board or get off the tracks because this train is taking us to the promised land."

"For?" Roscoe wasn't sure he wanted Abner on the map, he liked where it was, out of the way, unnoticed by outsiders.

"How about providing a nest egg to buy supplies for the safety team, new books for the library, or a sizable contribution to your rainy-day fund? The sky's the limit Mr. Chairman." While telling Roscoe about the benefits of his client coming to Abner, Rex removed a poster from his briefcase but kept the back to Roscoe.

Roscoe shook his head. "I think I missed something. Could we start..."

Before he could say, "over," Rex turned the poster around and said dramatically, "Introducing FeRoll, the most popular rapper in show business today. The kids in your community will go wild when they hear he's coming."

"FeRoll?" Roscoe repeated as he studied the figure on the poster. Something about him looked familiar. Although he was wearing a white headband that made the fur on his head stand up, and a tie-dyed tank top with, *Burn It To The Ground* printed on the front, something in the eyes gave him away. "That's Ferrel," he said with certainty. The last Roscoe heard, Ferrel, a longtime community member, was traveling with a theatrical company performing in *Les The Miser, None the Wiser.*

"No. No. No." Rex protested, waving his paws. "You've got the wrong guy."

Roscoe studied the poster and saw, beneath the picture of FeRoll with a gloved paw thrust in the air, part of the lyrics to the song he was singing. Or rapping. Or whatever.

Burn it to the g-round,
break it all a-part,
give folks in the co-mmun-i-ty
a brand new sta-art.
Uh-huh,
Throw the com-mit-tee.
in the str-eet,
and they'll re-mem-ber you,
the next time they me-et.

"Is that one of his songs?" Roscoe asked, pointing to the words on the poster.

Rex nodded enthusiastically. "Burn It to the Ground. Top of the charts baby, three weeks in a row. In this business, that's an eternity. It points out the corruption in community organizations starting at the top with the Committee of Committees."

"Things are going well. The best they have in years. Highly Exalted Chairman Cletus is doing a fantastic job. There's nothing to tear down." Roscoe didn't get it. But if Ferrel was FeRoll, he understood his distorted view of the world. He'd been a thorn in Roscoe's paw from the moment he became chairman.

"For those on the inside." Rex said as he walked to the small window above the wooden bench, pointed to the Clearing and asked, "What about out there, where the real members of the community live?"

Roscoe was about to say he grew up in Abner and you can't get more real than that but stopped when he heard a commotion outside. He crossed the room, stood next to Rex, and saw a group of seed school students walking up the path to the Clearing. He opened the window and heard,

"FeRoll,
is out of con-trol,
it don't take a poll,
to show
he is rea-dy to ro-oll.
Uh-huh.
He's coming to
our co-mmun-i-ty,
to sing the songs
that set us fre-ee."

Roscoe turned to Rex and asked, "Did you stop by seed school before coming here?"

"To ask for directions," Rex said innocently.

"Did you tell them why you're here?" Roscoe pressed the issue, although Rex looked like he was ready to move on.

"I may have mentioned it," he said as he put the poster of FeRoll back in his briefcase and was about to say he'd come back in a few days to iron out the details.

"And the poster they're carrying?" Roscoe pointed to the students marching around the tree the meeting room is in.

Rex looked through his briefcase and said, "I may have dropped a few on my way here."

In another part of the woods, Bigly Tweets studied the poster he'd found nailed to a tree announcing FeRoll's concert the coming weekend. He wouldn't have known who he was if it wasn't for his daughter, who knew the words to every song he sang. And if she did, so did the other kids in the woods who he was sure were begging their parents to let them go to the concert. It only cost a few seeds to get in but if enough kids came, it would provide a nice payday for him and his gang.

Finishing the thought was easy. When the concert started the seeds will be taken someplace to count and he had ways of finding out where. He turned to the two misfits he hung around with and said, "Huddle up boys, we have some work to do."

They moved closer, anxious to learn their part in Bigly's plan.

Harold looked up when Dawson knocked on the door frame before entering the security room. He kept the door open because there wasn't enough air movement to remove the heat coming from the wall of monitors. The problem was, those passing by saw it as an invitation to come in and visit.

"Big G called a meeting in five minutes," Dawson announced.

Harold gathered his things and asked, "In his office?"

Dawson shook his head, pointed to the floor and said, "Here."

Harold didn't understand why Big G insisted on meeting in the security room. It was the size of a large closet and the monitors on the wall, switching from one room to another made it difficult to concentrate on what he said. Those attending the meeting had to stand because there wasn't enough room for chairs. He wondered if Big G did it to keep the meetings short.

Soon, the room was filled with Big G managers, Officer Gardner, and Harold.

Big G pulled the stub of a cigar from his mouth, pointed at one of the monitors and asked, "What do you see?"

They'd been through this before and Harold wondered why he didn't tell them why they were there instead of making them guess. No one was going to come up with the answer he was looking for. After several unsuccessful tries, one of the managers pointed to a monitor and asked, "Are those the woods in back of the museum?"

Big G wiggled his fingers, encouraging him to say more.

The man mumbled something, then raised his hands, letting him know that was as far as he'd gone with the thought.

Big G pulled a marker from his pocket and wrote, *Shopping in the Woods*, across the surface of the monitor.

No one said anything because they didn't know what he was talking about.

"Shopping in the woods," he said slowly, tapping each word with the marker, leaving a series of black dots on the screen. He drew a circle in one part of the woods and wrote Dairy beneath it. Soon, canned goods and produce appeared next to other circles.

"What else?" he asked without turning around.

Quiet followed the question then the managers saw where he was going and offered, "Meat." "Poultry." And, "Bakery goods," with growing enthusiasm. After each answer, Big G drew a circle on the screen and wrote what they said beneath it.

"I don't understand," Harold said. "What's the point?"

Big G looked at the managers and said, "Did I ask for questions?"

"No sir." "Definitely not." "Not that I heard."

"Do I look like I'm interested in what he has to say?" After saying it Big G stuck the cigar in his mouth, put his hands on his hips, and glared at Harold.

"Not to me." "No interest whatsoever." "Not that I saw." From the managers.

He yanked the cigar from his mouth, pointed it at Harold and said, "You seem to have the impression want your, what's the buzzword going around today?" He snapped his fingers, asking the managers for the word.

"Data." "The big picture." "Input."

"That one. Input." Big G barked and chewed on his cigar before saying, "Well I don't. What I want is for you Finebender is to get behind the idea and make it happen. Right boys?"

"Yes sir." "Definitely." "Absolutely."

"If you hold an event outdoors this time of year, anything can happen. The weather could turn..." Before Harold could finish Big G wrote, "Shopping in snowmobiles," on the monitor.

"People driving vehicles in the woods raises serious liability issues," Harold tried to think of something to get him to abandon the event. "Your insurer might..."

Big G considered what he'd written, crossed out snowmobiles and replaced it with, "All-terrain vehicles."

"Great idea boss." "I can see it." "Shoppers will love it." The managers said enthusiastically.

Big G moved so he was standing in front of Harold, pointed the soggy end of the cigar at him and said angrily, "Instead of asking why, you should ask why not? I'm mixing things up. Turning a routine trip to the grocery store into an experience they'll never forget. I'll throw in free groceries for a month for the first person who gets an item from each area." He told Dawson to write that down. "Make married couples shop together. That will be a hoot. Contestants elbowing each other, fighting to be the first to cross the finish line."

Big G laughed.

The managers laughed with him.

He poked Harold in the chest with a beefy finger, said, "To make sure you're on board Finebender, I'm putting you in charge," and left the room. He was followed closely by the managers talking excitedly about all that needed to be done to pull off an event like this.   Selecting Harold to organize the event was not a spur of the moment decision. Since the turkey hunt, Big G felt something fishy was going on in the woods and was sure Harold Finebender, curator of the fountain pen museum, was at the center of it.

When they were alone Officer Gardner groaned, "He drew on the screen with a permanent marker. I sprayed it with cleaner, but it won't come off."

Harold stared at the top of his desk, trying to figure out what to do. He didn't care if Big G's plan worked or not, he was concerned about the squirrels and how an event like *Shopping in the Woods* would disrupt their lives. Trees would have to be removed to make paths wide enough for the vehicles and the work the squirrels had done to get the woods the way they wanted would be destroyed.

Harold drove home with thoughts of how to warn them about what was coming swirling in his head. He picked at the food on his plate at supper and went to bed before the ten o'clock news but couldn't sleep. He tossed and turned so much Thelma told him if he didn't move to the recliner in the family room she would.

Shortly after the newspaper hit the front step, he had an idea. It wasn't the answer he was hoping for, one that made the problem go away, but it would let the squirrels know what was coming and give them a chance to prepare for it.

When he arrived at work, he bypassed his usual trip to Penultimate and went straight to the security room. He took a picture of the monitor Big G wrote on with the woods in the background, sent it to the printer, and was pleased with the results. He stuck the copy he'd made among other papers on his clipboard and walked to Dawson's office. He's the *Manager of Special Projects* and Big G told him to work with Harold on the *Shopping in the Woods* event.

Soon they were in the woods, marking trees to be removed and staking out areas where products would be displayed. As they were leaving, Harold dropped the print he'd made of the marks on the monitor near the stump of a tree. That was the best he could do. If he did more, Dawson would report it to his boss.

It was up to the squirrels now.

Members of the *Committee for the Protection of Neighborhood Resources* stood around the conference table, watching Webster make notes as he studied the picture Seed Man dropped in the woods. Finally, he sat back and said, "I've figured out what's going on and it's not good."

Committee members took their seats and Webster told them they were looking at a picture of the woods and someone planned to sell groceries there.

His explanation raised more questions than it answered. "Why would humans put groceries here?" "Will customers come in the morning or afternoon?" And most importantly, "What are groceries?" Webster reminded them since they voted to meet here and not in the library, the *Dictionary of Human Markings and What They Mean* wasn't available.

One member pounded the table with his paw and declared, "That does it. Little by little we're losing territory. It's time to take back the woods." Webster told him that was a good idea but impossible to pull off. In case he hadn't noticed, they were outnumbered.

Dorman asked where the picture came from. Webster told him Emmet was on guard duty and saw Seed Man and another human walking around, putting marks on the ground. As they were leaving, Seed Man dropped it near the stump of a tree.

Dorman thought for a moment, then nodded like he'd figured out what was going on. "He's sending a message."

Webster agreed but felt they needed more than a picture to understand what the message was.

Dorman expressed the fears of others on the committee when he asked, "What are we going to do Mr. Chairman? The woods will be full of humans, there won't be room for us."

Roscoe put a paw on his shoulder and said, "We have some time before the event, we'll think of something."

Roscoe had an early meeting with the zoning board of the Committee of Committees and made it as far as the big rock that separates the community of Abner from Ben when he remembered he'd left a document he needed in the meeting room. He hurried back, went inside, and found Ferrel standing by the small window above the wooden bench.

"Ferrel?" he said in surprise.

Ferrel waited a moment before saying, "It's like I never left."

"I'm sorry?" Roscoe was only half listening. He found the document he needed and was writing a note to Megan reminding her he'd be gone most of the morning.

"I've been away three months and nothing's changed." There was a note of melancholy in his voice.

"Not in three months but things are..."

"The library, the safety training room, and seed school are where they were when I left." His voice trailed off.

Roscoe remained silent, sure Ferrel wasn't interested in what he had to say. Talk about things not changing.

"I've traveled the world Roscoe, performed before huge crowds. Heard my name, my stage name, repeated by," he hesitated, trying to pick a number large enough to impress but not so large he wouldn't believe it, "hundreds of adoring fans."

Roscoe started toward the door thinking he could leave and it wouldn't make any difference. He stopped when Ferrel asked, "How are the kids?"

His son Ferrel Jr. was joined to Penny, Roscoe's daughter. "They're great. Ferrel Jr. works at the post office and is responsible for keeping the sorting equipment running. Darin says if he wasn't there to fix things when they break, the mail wouldn't be delivered on time." Roscoe hesitated before saying, "Penny's expecting."

Ferrel took in the news, nodded, and said, "I stopped by my nest. Wilma wasn't there."

"Her father is ill, she's gone to take care of him," Roscoe explained.

Ferrel realized things had changed. On the surface they looked the same but underneath, where community members lived, it was a different story. "I see," he mumbled as he stepped away from the window. "I see," he repeated as he walked out of the meeting room without closing the door.

As Roscoe took the path to the COC he noticed unusual looking equipment located in different parts of the woods. There was a display case, Styrofoam coolers, and tables designed to hold fruit and vegetables. He made the connection between the picture Seed

Man left for them and the equipment. He smiled and knew what the community could do to put an end to the problem.

Shopping in the Woods was scheduled to start at eight in the morning, but the parking lot was full by six. Those who arrived early were treated to coffee and mama G's double dipped doughnuts, compliments of Big G Grocery. A number turned down the offer, choosing to spend the time stretching, or sprinting across the field. When they reached the woods, they were stopped by members of the Centerline Home Guard, stationed there to keep contestants from gaining an advantage by looking at the course.

Harold's concern about bad weather was unnecessary, it was a beautiful morning. There'd been frost on the field when the first shoppers arrived, but as the sun rose, it burned off before the contest started.

Big G watched from his office. He'd sent his managers out to mingle with the crowd, pass out discount coupons, and explain to the media what was going on. He chewed contentedly on his cigar and thought of the free publicity he'd received in the past week.

A digital clock in the parking lot counted down the time. Thirty minutes before the start, contestants were relaxed and chatting with one another. At five minutes they grew serious and began inching their all-terrain vehicles closer to the starting line.

Pedestrians on the sidewalk in front of the museum heard motors revving, and shouts of frustration from those whose vehicles wouldn't start.

Finally, the clock flashed zero and with a roar the contestants shot across the field toward the woods.

Members of the home guard, expecting to hear a starters gun or the blast of an air horn to start the event, scrambled to get out of the way of the approaching vehicles.

Lights strung from trees in the woods came on directing the shoppers to various locations to pick up produce or seafood products. To win the event, a contestant had to get an item from each area.

Once in the woods, vehicles crashed into trees, dazing the drivers, and knocking them out of the competition. Several racing to be the first to reach a product area, refused to back down as they sped down the narrow paths and were swallowed up by bushes and underbrush.

The first shopper to enter the woods followed the lights to the dairy section. He skidded to a stop in front of a refrigerated cabinet. His partner jumped out to grab a bottle of milk or tub of margarine. Thoughts filled the driver's mind of what he would do with the money he saved by not buying groceries for a month. Concerned they were losing time, he honked the horn when he saw his partner looking frantically through a refrigerated cabinet.

"What's wrong?" He shouted over the roar of a second vehicle entering the area. His partner lifted his hands and shook his head.

"What?" the driver asked as he watched his chance for a quick getaway blocked by a third vehicle.

The sound of vehicles entering the area made it hard for him to hear his partner's answer. "There's nothing there," he said as he climbed in the vehicle, thinking someone got there before he did.

The driver forced his way through a narrow opening, scraping a fender against another vehicle and causing a crack to streak across his windshield. Then they were off to another location, skidding around curves and taking corners on two wheels. When they arrived at the *Seafood* area, they saw contestants standing in front of an empty cooler.

They shared their experience at other locations and concluded there were no groceries, they were the victims of another of Big G's practical jokes.

"Big G Grocery Zero for Two," was the lead story by every news anchor in the city. A screen in back of them showed teams racing across the field, heading for the woods. As it played the announcer said solemnly, "The needn't have hurried because there were no groceries. Shame on Big G for putting shoppers in harm's way for a few laughs." The last shot the viewer saw before the station shifted to the weather forecast, was a contestant walking aimlessly in the field between the woods and the museum, dazed after his vehicle collided with a tree.

So many turned out for the *Burn It to the Ground* concert it was moved from the gymnasium to the parade field behind the school. Parents carried the stage from the gymnasium to the field. They had no trouble seeing where they were going because the lights from *Shopping in the Woods* were still on.

When Rex felt the crowd was growing restless, he put a paw on Ferrel's shoulder and whispered, "Show time."

Ferrel ran up the steps, across the platform and struck the pose everyone in the crowd recognized from magazine articles and album covers. It looked like he was taking a step, one leg straight, the other bent. His body leaned forward as he thrust a gloved paw in the air.

He held the pose, and the crowd went wild. Younger members screamed and chanted "FeRoll. FeRoll."

When he felt emotions were at their peak, he spun around and started the performance with *Face Time,* a song from *Bring It!* his latest album. The crowd sang along with him.

"Look me in the fa-ace,
say I don't be-long.
Talk about my at-ti-tude,
don't know right from ..."

He hesitated. It took a few seconds for the crowd to realize he'd stopped; some had gone to the second verse. They were rapping with him, waving their paws in the air, and stomping their feet in time with the music.

He started over and got as far as be-long before stopping. Those closer to the stage looked around, thinking he did it on purpose, getting the crowd pumped up.

A member of the cleaning crew at the fountain pen museum noticed someone left the lights for *Shopping in the Woods* on. He flipped the switch, turning them off. The only illumination at the parade field came from a single spotlight Rex directed at the performer.

Ferrel stood motionless for a moment, then removed the headband and used it to wipe makeup from his face. The crowd was so quiet they could hear traffic on the street in front of the Seed Man's building.

Younger members didn't know what to do. They hadn't been to a FeRoll concert and didn't want to be uncool and do something stupid. At the same time, it was kind of embarrassing.

The silence was broken when Ferrel, with no pre-recorded accompaniment, began singing *Finding My Way Home*, the final song from *Les The Miser None The Wiser*. Older members of the community moved closer to the stage, drawn by the melancholy words and Ferrel's clear tenor voice.

"I walk down unfamiliar streets,

abandoned and alone,

then a path appears,

I follow it,

and suddenly... I'm home."

As the last words of the song echoed through the woods, Ferrel stood with his head down, his arms at his side. He didn't want the crowd to see the tears streaming down his face. Older community member began to applaud. Others joined them.

Rex had been in show business long enough to know timing was everything so when the applause reached its peak, he turned off the spotlight.

Bigly Tweets stood at the back of the crowd thinking about the bonanza that would have been his if Principal Charles hadn't announced the concert was free, Ferrel's gift to the community.

He shrugged and walked away, baffled by the whole concert thing. His friends waited to see if there would be an encore before following him.

Monday morning Harold punched the code on the keypad. When he opened the door to the security room, he saw Big G sitting in Officer Gardner's chair, staring at a monitor on the wall. He'd pulled up a video of Dawson and him walking toward the woods. He saw himself point to the right, then move his arm to the left. Dawson nodded and wrote something in his notebook. They moved out of camera range for a second and when they reappeared, they were on their way back to the museum, talking about all that had to done before the day for the event arrived.

Big G stared at the screen, chewed his cigar, rewound the film and watched it again, looking for anything that would provide an answer to what went wrong with his *Shopping In The Woods* idea and the role Harold played in ruining it.

Harold backed out of the room and closed the door. Officer Gardner had completed his rounds and was walking toward the security room to file his hourly report. He stopped when Harold pointed to the second floor and made a gesture like he was drinking a cup of coffee. Officer Gardner nodded and joined him on his way to Penultimate.

In the woods, members of the community of Abner had formed a line and were passing the food they'd taken from the coolers and display cases to one another. They stacked it at the edge of the road near the pond. When the last item was placed on the pile, Roscoe sent Sheldon to the library to let Webster know they were ready.

Webster left the library, walked to the edge of the road, and stuck a sign in the ground next to the groceries that read, "hep U sef."

HAPPY TRAILS TO YOU

Part 1: Until We Meet Again

Roscoe was halfway up the steps to the meeting room when he stopped to catch his breath. He woke up with a scratchy throat but after getting out of bed and moving around, he felt better.

Now he wasn't sure. He wondered if he should go back to his nest and take a personal day off.

When his breathing returned to normal, he entered the room and walked to his desk where Megan had placed several items for his attention. There was a reminder that she was helping her parents move to the senior center and would be late for work. A note from Webster let him know the latest Inspector BaGel book was in. He'd set it aside but could only hold it a few days, it wouldn't be long before others found out it was there.

There was also a letter from the Committee of Committees saying Abner was a finalist for the *Community of Excellence* award. It went on to explain a team would arrive in a few days to complete the evaluation process. Roscoe studied the names of those on the team but didn't recognize anyone. He guessed he was getting old, he used to know everyone at the COC.

He decided to go to the library and get the book before his day became too busy. He stood to leave, felt dizzy, and put a paw on his desk to steady himself. He waited for the feeling to pass before walking across the Clearing to the library. When he entered, he waved to Webster letting him know he'd come to pick up the book.

Webster returned the greeting, stepped in the storage room and returned with the book still in the box it came in. He left it that way so a volunteer wouldn't record its arrival and put it on the *New Books* shelf. He said, "Here you go Rosc..." then, seeing him clinging to the edge of the checkout desk with his eyes closed and his face drained of color asked, "Are you okay?"

He helped him to a chair in the reading area. Earlier in the month the COC sent an all-community letter saying because of the mild winter and wet spring, squirrel fever season arrived earlier than usual and urged everyone to take precautions. A flyer with *What To Do To Avoid Squirrel Fever* on the cover was attached to the letter. Despite taking precautions, Roscoe had picked up the virus.

Webster was looking for someone to send for Doc when he heard a thump, turned, and saw Roscoe sprawled on the floor.

When members of the *Committee for the Protection of Neighborhood Resources* heard Roscoe would be out for a few days, they huddled in the meeting room and selected Clifford to be his replacement when the *Community of Excellence* team arrived. They chose him because he worked for the community maintaining the trails in the woods and could be available at a moment's notice. His father, also named Clifford, had the job before him. He'd refused to add the second, or junior to his son's name claiming, "I'm old, he's young. I don't see a problem." When he went the way of all squirrels, the committee gave the job of trail maintenance to his son.

To say he maintained the trails is an understatement. Trails were his passion. He formed the *Ancient Trails Society* to uncover trails left by those who lived in the woods before the community of Abner arrived.

Another reason for selecting Clifford was, it got them off the hook for doing the job.

JR checked the list of things Sparky wanted done while he was gone. He's Roscoe and Penny Sue's son, and Penny's twin brother. Penny followed her interest in education and taught first years at seed school until being joined to Ferrel Jr., they're expecting their first child.

JR chose science. While in seed school he spent every spare moment at Sparky's lab, learning all he could from the master. After graduating, he went to the Science Academy and made such an impression on the faculty they asked him to stay and teach.

He'd taken time off to do research for a book he was writing on a more efficient way to store acorns when a letter from Sparky arrived asking if he would serve as technical advisor for the community while he was away at a conference. JR saw it as a win-win situation, he'd get to spend time with his parents, be there for the birth of his niece or nephew, and fiddle around in Sparky's lab. If there was time, he'd work on his book at the library. At Sparky's urging, Webster created a *Science and Technology* section and filled it with books he recommended.

He chuckled when he saw the first thing on Sparky's list of things to do was test the quality of water in the pond and record the results in the *Water Purity Logbook*. The pond is the main source of water for the community, so making sure it was safe to drink was crucial. He wondered how long Sparky had been doing this, it was one of his jobs when he worked for him during the summer break at seed school. He flipped back through the pages of the logbook and smiled when he came to an entry with his initials in the *Recorded By* column.

At the top of each page was the familiar SCAR system Sparky created for evaluating water samples. He was to check for Sediment, Clarity, and any unusual Activity before filing a Report.

He'd dipped the test tube in the water to collect a sample when he noticed a dead fish caught in the branches of a bush at the edge of the pond. He put on the latex gloves Sparky kept in the water testing kit, along with tweezers, a notebook, two pencils, and an extra test tube in case something happened to the one in use. He'd lifted the fish from the water and was examining it when he heard voices coming from the path leading to the pond.

He gathered his equipment and stepped behind a tree when three community members left the path and walked toward the pond. Two looked like students and the third their teacher. It could be three students he thought, the one explaining something as they walked along didn't look old enough to be a teacher. He thought of Miss Mabel who taught *Cultural Trends In Communities* so long, her students carried her to her classroom when she could no longer make it to the second floor on her own.

When they reached the edge of the pond, the one in charge showed the students how to take a water sample without getting any on their paws. While the water in the pond was probably okay, taking precautions was always a good practice. Who knew what they'd find if, after graduating, they were responsible for the water supply of another community.

The students withdrew a tube from their test kit and dipped it in the water. They put a cork in the open end as she'd instructed, held it to the light, and recorded what they saw. The teacher took a closer look at the samples then said something to them. They gathered their things and went back to school while she went in a different direction.

JR left his hiding place, sprinted through the woods, opened the door to Sparky's lab, and stepped inside. He didn't know what to do with the fish he was holding but couldn't keep it in the lab, it was starting to smell. He opened the door to throw it out and bumped into the one he saw at the pond.

"Sparky?" she asked in surprise. The person who opened the door didn't look old enough to have done all the things she'd heard about.

JR shook his head and explained he was looking after things while Sparky was away, he didn't see any reason to explain why Sparky picked him. Besides, he was having trouble concentrating on what she said, she was beautiful.

She stuck out a paw and said, "I'm Rebecca. To my students I'm Ms. Rebecca but my friends call me Beck."

"You're a teacher?" JR asked as they touched paws and immediately felt foolish, didn't she say she had students?

"We were taking samples at the pond and got some unusual results. I was going to ask Sparky to take a look but since he's not here..." She shrugged and turned to go.

"I'll do it," JR said the first thing that popped in his head, anything to keep her here a little longer.

"Do you know how to operate the equipment?" she asked, skeptically.

He told her he'd done it before and invited her inside, thinking they could test the sample together.

"I'll take a rain check, I have to get back to my class," she told him and turned to go.

"I'm, ah, going to the library. I'll walk with you." JR wasn't good at this. He hadn't shown much interest in females when he attended seed school, science occupied his thoughts. When he went to the academy his time was taken up with studies, he'd doubled the load so he would finish faster. Teaching required time to put lesson plans together, as did setting up experiments, so there wasn't room in his schedule for dating.

"Afraid I'll get lost?" she asked playfully.

"No," he said quietly, "I'm afraid I will."

She looked at him, not sure what to make of the comment. She pointed to the fish he was holding and said, "If you're bringing that with you, I'd rather go alone."

JR dropped the fish in the mailbox by the door, he'd take care of it later. He hadn't been aware he was holding it; he couldn't stop looking into her beautiful blue eyes.

In the time he'd spent at Sparky's lab, JR couldn't remember spending the night here. Regardless of how late they worked on a project, Sparky would say, "It's time for you to go, I don't want your parents to worry." So, it felt strange to climb the ladder to the loft above the entrance and stretch out on a mattress filled with synthetic straw Sparky invented. He'd tried to convince community members to use it when building their nests, pointing out its long life and ability to shed water after a heavy rain, but he couldn't get them to change what they were used to. He didn't know if Sparky ever slept up here. When he'd stop by on his way to school, he'd find him asleep at the workbench where he'd been conducting an experiment or curled up under a chalkboard filled with calculations.

He thought about how fortunate he'd been to have spent time with Sparky, no other community had anyone like him. They had members who could fix things, but not invent them. He was about to doze off when he heard a beeping sound. He climbed down the ladder and looked around the lab, thinking he forgot to turn something off. Everything was in order, so he walked to the door, opened it, and found the sound louder outside.

He followed the path that ended at the pond and saw a pickup truck parked so it couldn't be seen from the road behind the woods. The beeping continued as the truck backed toward the pond. When it stopped the driver got out, grabbed a rake from the bed of the truck, and cleared an area of leaves and dead grass.

When he finished, he leaned the rake against a tree, bent down, and pushed a sheet of plywood to one side revealing a large hole. He went back to the truck, lifted a plastic container from the back and dumped the contents in the hole.

JR didn't know how the human could stand to be so close, he was on the opposite side of the pond and the smell was overpowering.

The human emptied two more containers in the hole. When he finished, he put the plywood back in place, and scattered leaves over it. He tossed the rake and the empty containers in the back of the truck, climbed in, and drove away, using the parking lights. When he reached the road, he turned on the headlights providing enough light for JR to see *Big G Grocery* on the side of the truck.

Harold walked from the museum to his car. Unlike most days since Big G took over today had been uneventful. No emergency meetings to discuss ways to improve sales or department managers interrupting phone calls to ask where something in the building was located. He sniffed the air as he got closer to his car and wondered what was in the dumpster that smelled so bad.

He opened the door to his car and discovered the smell wasn't coming from the dumpster but from inside his car. Specifically, the small package in the front seat. He looked around, thinking one of Big G's managers had played a practical joke on him. Big G would like nothing better than for him to get fed up and quit. He decided if they were going to do stuff like this, he'd stop leaving the windows partially open to prevent heat from buildup up when the sun was on the parking lot side of the building.

He picked the package up with two fingers, carried it to the dumpster and tossed it in. He was about to return to his car when he saw a squirrel standing with his back against a side of the dumpster, looking at him. When he was sure Harold saw him, he put a paw to his lips and pointed at the camera on the back of the building.

Harold nodded he understood.

The squirrel dropped a piece of paper on the ground and shoved it toward Harold with his foot. It was the note Lloyd stuck on the back of the camera he left in the woods in case someone saw it and wondered what it was doing there.

Harold picked the paper up and saw *Lloyd Brewster, Big G Grocery, Jackson Hollow.* Jackson Hollow is one of several small communities in Centerline along with Malcolm's Ridge, and Griffin Park West.

Aware the camera was recording his movements, he wadded up the paper, tossed it in the dumpster, walked to his car, and reluctantly got in. Although the source was gone, the smell remained, so he rolled down the windows as he pulled out of his parking space.

On his way back from delivering the note to Seed Man, JR stopped by the meeting room to see how things were going and learned two committee members had the same symptoms his father had. He was about to leave when he asked Megan if his father served tea at the last committee meeting. It had become a tradition for members to hang around when a meeting was over to discuss the decisions they'd made over a cup of walnut tea.

She wasn't sure, but said he probably did. She looked in the closet and found the kettle he'd used to heat the water. There was some liquid in the bottom, and she was looking for a rag to dry it when he told her he'd take it the way it was.

Harold wasn't sure where the Big G Grocery in Jackson Hollow was, so he drove around until he found it. He lives on the other side of town and seldom came here. He found a parking space, got out, and joined others entering the store.

Once inside, he approached an employee stocking shelves, explained he was looking for Lloyd Brewster, and asked if she knew where he was. Without looking up, she pointed toward the ceiling.

Harold gasped, overcome by the news. "You mean he's... passed on?" If he had, why did the squirrel give him the paper with his name on it?

The employee stopped what she was doing and gave him a look that asked how he came up with that? "His shift is over. He lives in the apartment above the store." She shook her head and went back to putting cans of green beans on a shelf.

With the help of another employee, Harold found the door to Lloyd's apartment and knocked, not sure what to expect. When it opened, he was facing a young man who looked like he was still in high school. He wore a T-shirt with a picture of a solar eclipse on the front, cut-off jeans, and sandals with no socks. He was thin and the round lenses of his glasses gave him a scholarly look.

Now that he'd found him, he wasn't sure what to say. "Lloyd Brewster?" he asked. Lloyd looked like he was upset he'd stopped what he was doing to find a salesman at the door or worse, the manager with a problem.

"This is going to sound strange but... a squirrel gave me a card with your name on it." Harold braced for laughter and a door slammed in his face. Instead, Lloyd looked behind him to make sure no one was watching and pulled him inside. Harold followed him up a flight of stairs and down a narrow hallway until they came to a door. He opened it and Harold couldn't believe what he saw; every surface had a catalog or a box of electronic parts on it. On a workbench he saw parts of a computer he was putting together.

After clearing a place for him to sit, Lloyd asked, "What's this about a squirrel?"

Harold started from the beginning, explained how he moved the squirrels from his backyard to the woods behind the museum. From time to time, he took them home and brought them back the next morning.

During the explanation, Lloyd listened with an intensity Harold found unnerving.

When he finished, Lloyd hesitated, wondering if he could trust this stranger who showed up at his door. There were rumors Big G did this, sent someone in disguise to test an employee's loyalty. He decided to take a chance and share how he stopped two trouble making kids from attacking an injured squirrel and playing an unusual game of tic-tac-toe. He put a camera in a tree to see who his opponent was. The card the squirrel gave him was the one he put on the camera in case someone found it and wondered what it was doing there.

When Beck finished the last class of the day, she gathered her things and was about to leave when JR entered her room and asked, "You got a minute?"

"That depends on what you have in mind?" she said coyly.

"Come to the lab. I tested the samples you left and got some unusual results. I'd like you to check my work."

Beck thought that was the most unusual pickup line she'd heard but, after thinking it over said, "Sure. Why not?" She wasn't about to mention she'd been looking for a chance to see him again.

They were almost to the lab when JR, while describing the procedures he'd followed analyzing the samples, mentioned performing the Glickman test. She stopped walking, studied him for a moment and asked, "What test?"

He was stuck. He'd hoped to be more low key, saving his background until he got to know her better. But the seed was out of the feeder, so he decided to get it over with. "I studied under Professor Glickman at the Science Academy. He added a final test to rule out errors caused by sloppy sample collecting technique." He was afraid learning his background would scare her away.

She chuckled quietly. She'd done some research of her own and knew who he was and where he went to school. After making him promise to show the procedure to her class, she grabbed his paw and said, "Let's go."

When they reached the lab, he went through the series of tests that made a connection between what the human dumped in the hole by the pond and the sample from the kettle he took from the meeting room.

"So, it's polluted water not squirrel fever?" she asked, thinking out loud. "Several of my students have become ill and missed school."

There was an uncomfortable moment that was broken when Beck said, "What do you say we start over?" She stuck out her paw and said, "I'm Beck and teach science at seed school."

JR didn't know what to say until she poked him in the arm and said in a teasing way, "Lighten up JR, it's not a difficult question."

Clifford was at the conference table in the meeting room studying a map his father made. He ran a finger along a trail that ended abruptly. His father called it the *Mystery Trail* and spent years searching for it but, as far as Clifford knew, never found where it ended.

It took two tries for Megan to get his attention. When he looked up, she introduced the *Community of Excellence* team but wasn't sure he'd stopped thinking about the map he was looking at. After a few uncomfortable moments he blinked, stood, and said, "I'm Clifford, welcome to Abner." They gave him a copy of the agenda they planned to follow and told him they hadn't a moment to lose, they were visiting another community in the afternoon.

Harold was surprised to find he was whistling as he walked from his car to the museum. He felt a burden had been lifted from his shoulders. He'd been the lone champion for the squirrels in the woods then, out of the blue, he found a soul mate, someone as passionate about their safety and wellbeing as he was.

He was looking forward to the day as he punched in the code on the keypad, opened the door to the security room, and found Big G sitting at his desk.

Officer Gardner was at the computer terminal with his hands on the keyboard. He didn't look up when Harold entered, sure if he did, he'd see the look of disappointment on his face.

"Better late than never," Big G growled then to Officer Gardner, "Roll it."

Officer Gardner touched the button on the mouse and Harold found he was looking at the dumpster. He watched as he walked to his car, stepped back and turned his head like he smelled something awful. He removed a package from the front seat of his car, tossed it in the dumpster, and was about to walk away when he stopped to pick a scrap of paper off the ground. He looked at it then threw it in the dumpster.

Big G shouted, "Stop!"

Officer Gardner did.

Big G studied Harold for a moment before asking, "What kind of game are you playing Finebender?"

While searching for an answer, Harold glanced at the monitor that had switched back to real time and saw Lloyd Brewster leave the parking lot and ride across the field on his bicycle. It happened so fast, if you weren't looking, you'd miss it. If you were, it looked like a neighborhood kid on his way to spend the morning exploring the woods. The moment he reached the woods, he was out of camera range.

Officer Gardner saw it but didn't react.

Big G studied Harold's face, looking for a sign that he was the culprit behind the two failed promotions in the woods, so he missed it.

Before Harold could answer Big G said, "After you left, I had Dawson go through the dumpster, looking for the package you put there." He looked over his half glasses and said, "He found a fish."

The thought of Dawson in his expensive suit, climbing around in a dumpster full of trash made Harold smile.

"You think this is funny Finebender? That your attempt to destroy my reputation is a joke?" Big G shouted.

Harold shook his head. "Not at all." He turned from the monitor, looked Big G in the eye and said, "I wasn't going to say anything but since the *Shopping in the Woods* disaster, I have received... threats. At first, they were notes stuck under my windshield wiper. But lately," he pointed to the monitor, letting him know the threat level had increased, the fish in his car was an example.

"Gardner!" Big G grunted and Officer Gardner dropped his head, like he'd rather be anyplace but here, making things worse for Harold by the minute. He rewound the film to earlier in the day. Harold saw his car in his parking space. Occasionally someone visiting the museum parked next to it, went on the tour, returned, and drove away.

Just as a car was going by there was a splash of color and a package sailed through the partially open window of his car.

"Stop!" Big G demanded. "Back it up! Easy does it," he ordered and when the film reached the place where the package went through the window he said, "Enlarge!"

When Officer Gardner did, Harold saw what looked like the paw of a squirrel. Then the car went by and whatever had been there was gone. "There's your prankster," Big G said with a laugh, grew serious and added "you've been squirreled." He got up, threw what was left of his cigar in a wastebasket, and walked out of the room laughing.

Lloyd got off his bike and leaned it against a tree at the entrance to the woods. He wasn't sure why he'd come. Was the squirrel sending a message for help when he gave Mr. Finebender the card he put on the camera? Or, if after their meeting, his imagination took over. He was thinking about that when he entered the woods and almost tripped over a squirrel standing in the middle of the path like he was waiting for him. When he was sure Lloyd saw him, JR moved a few feet away and stopped. Lloyd followed and soon was jogging to keep up with his guide as they raced through the woods. They stopped when they reached a pond Lloyd hadn't seen when he was here before. He wondered if this was what the squirrel wanted him to see.

It wasn't.

His guide continued to the other side of the pond where a group of squirrels were waiting. By the time Lloyd got there, they'd removed enough debris to reveal a sheet of plywood. He started to lift the panel to see what was beneath it but let go after raising it a few inches, the smell was overpowering. He recognized it as rotting fat, trimmed from slabs of beef. He was familiar with the smell; it was in the air when there'd been a power outage at the store and he was asked to get the meat locker running again.

The one who led him to the pond, moved away and stood where bent grass revealed the tracks of a vehicle. Lloyd followed them until they reached the road and guessed this was the route the driver took when he brought the rancid products to dump in the hole.

Big G finished a phone call, removed an imported cigar from the humidor he kept in a drawer of his desk, and unwrapped it as he walked to the window. He loved the view from here. In one direction he could see the top of the taller buildings in downtown Centerline. In the other, the sight of the green field, and the variety of trees in the woods never failed to calm his mind. He leaned closer to the window when he saw a bicycle being pushed into the woods by... squirrels?

He dialed Dawson's number and shouted, "My office! Now!"

Dawson arrived, gasping for breath after running up the stairs. Big G told him to, "Go to the woods and look around, something funny is going on."

The moment Dawson stepped in the woods a signal was sent by the guard on duty. It passed from nest to nest, through the Clearing and on to the squirrels at the pond. They quickly covered the plywood with leaves and disappeared. Lloyd wasn't sure what was going on until the one who brought him here stepped behind a tree and motioned for him to follow.

He understood why when a human in a suit, white shirt and tie staggered to the edge of the pond. A pocket of his suit coat was torn, and cockleburs covered the legs of his trousers. A glob of mud was stuck to the toe of his once shiny shoe. He wiped perspiration from his face with a monogrammed handkerchief and, not sure what he was supposed to be looking for mumbled, "Whatever," then plunged back through the woods, searching for the path that brought him there.

When Lloyd thought it was safe, he stepped from behind the tree and saw the squirrel he'd followed, holding a camera in his paw. He recognized it as the one he used to catch the kids who knocked the squirrel out of the tree. He nodded when he figured out what the squirrel wanted, climbed the tree they'd hidden behind, and placed the camera so it was aimed at the spot where the sheet of plywood covered the hole in the ground. He turned it on and was pleased when a small green light came on, letting him know the battery still had power.

The *Community of Excellence* team left seed school, impressed by what they saw. The students were eager to learn, and the teachers were doing their best to help them succeed. They were halfway to the meeting room when Clifford stopped, looked at the trees around them, smacked his forehead with a paw said, "You idiot. The top of the trees not the bottom," and walked away, studying the gaps in the treetops.

The team didn't know what to do. They were in unfamiliar territory with no idea how to get back to the meeting room. When they heard the signal to take cover, they looked to the one in charge to tell them what to do. They barely made it under the branch of an evergreen before a human stumbled in their direction. He went deeper in the woods and moments later they heard him grumbling as he crashed through the underbrush, going back in the direction he'd come.

When the all clear sounded, they sighed with relief until they realized their situation hadn't changed, they were as lost as they were before the human showed up.

They jumped with surprise when someone asked, "Can I help you?" and were relieved when they saw JR standing a few feet away. They told him who they were, how Clifford had abandoned them, and they didn't know how to get back to the meeting room where they left their things. JR said he'd take them and along the way, told them what it was like growing up in Abner and why it was such a special place for him.

He dropped them off when they reached the Clearing where Megan was waiting on the platform outside the meeting room.

She'd worn a groove in the floor from her desk to the small window over the wooden bench looking for them. She was relieved when they entered the meeting room, apologized for Clifford's behavior, and told them about a shortcut that would get them to the other community on time.

As they gathered their things the one in charge said she hadn't had a chance to thank the young fellow who brought them here. When Megan asked who it was, she said she thought his name was, "JB or JP, something like that."

Megan promised she'd tell him the next time she saw him and thought the acorn didn't fall far from the tree. In the time he'd spent with them, JR hadn't mentioned he was the chairman's son.

Dawson made it back to the museum and stopped at the men's room to comb his hair and repair his torn clothing before reporting to Big G. He leaned toward the mirror and pressed a damp cloth against a bruise on his cheek, received when he collided with a low hanging branch.

He left the bathroom, limped up the stairs with a knee swollen to the size of a cantaloupe, and knocked on Big G's door.

Big G sat somberly in his chair, listening while Dawson gave his report. "You found nothing?" Big G asked and wondered if he'd sent the right guy to find out what was going on.

Dawson shook his head and would like to have said it would have helped if he knew what he was looking for. Aware of the mood Big G was in, he decided to keep his thoughts to himself.

Neither of them was close enough to the window to see a boy leave the woods on his bicycle and pedal across the parking lot. He'd pulled on the street and merged with the traffic when Big G walked to the window and looked at the woods. Something was going on there, he could feel it. He vowed to find out what it was if he had to go there and do it himself.

Harold didn't know what to think of the message he received on his phone that said a prescription was ready for pick up at the Big

G pharmacy at Jackson Hollow. He read it again, sure they'd sent it to the wrong person. If he had a prescription to fill, he'd take it to Midlands, a drug store near his house. Finally, it sunk in. It wasn't just any Big G store it was the one where Lloyd Brewster worked.

He swung by the store on his way home and pulled in the parking lot. He approached the pharmacist and gave his name. He went through sacks filed alphabetically in a bin and slowed when he reached the F section. "Ferguson," he mumbled quietly to himself, "Finch." He stopped when he came to Finebender, handed the package to him, and said, "There's no charge, your insurance covers it."

Harold thanked him and as he left the store, wondered what was going on. He hadn't been to a doctor recently and his insurance didn't cover prescriptions.

When he was safely in his car, he opened the sack, but instead of pills in the plastic bottle, he found a thumb drive for the USB port on his computer. "Open immediately," was written on the label glued to the bottle. He saw it had been ordered by L. Brewster.

When he got home, he went straight to his office, turned on the computer, and inserted the flash drive. He looked in the directory, found the port the thumb drive was in and hit open. Although it was shot at night, he could make out a Big G truck backing across the grass and stopping near a pond. The film continued but Harold was only half watching, he was thinking of how to get the information in the right hands without Big G discovering he was the whistle-blower.

Officer Gardner met Traci Kline, investigative reporter at *Centerline Morning*, the local newspaper, at the entrance to the museum, and took her to a conference room where Harold was waiting. He motioned for her to sit down and asked if she'd like a cup of coffee. She did and Officer Gardner left to get it.

They exchanged small talk until he returned, set a cup for each of them on the table, then left to stand guard in the hall outside the conference room. When it was just the two of them, Harold got down to business. "We're putting together an exhibit for the pen used to settle the dispute between Gludistan and Galvonia."

Traci closed her notebook and said, "That's old news. The deal fell through, they're still at war."

Harold slid a piece of paper toward her that explained the reason he asked to see her had nothing to do with the conflict or the pen exhibit. He had a thumb drive he thought she would find interesting. He waited for her to read the note. When she finished, he wadded it up, threw it in the wastebasket, then launched into the story of how the pen came to be in his possession. He'd just dropped the thumb drive in her purse when he heard Big G tell Officer Gardner, "Get out of my way or you'll be guarding the dumpster the rest of your life," before bursting into the room with Dawson close behind. He stopped at the table where they were sitting, removed the cigar from his mouth, looked at Harold and growled, "Who is she and what's she doing here?"

Harold introduced Traci to Big G and explained she was writing an article about the pen from Galvonia. He was providing background information.

"It's a fascinating story," Traci said, "my readers will love it." She gathered the papers Harold gave her about the conflict, the date of the program, and that Ambassador Given would make a few comments before officially donating the pen to the museum.

"Hold your horses," Big G growled as he took the papers from her, gave them to Dawson and told him to, "Check 'um out."

Not knowing what he was looking for, Dawson studied the front and back of each page before giving them back to Big G and saying, "They look okay to me sir."

Big G tossed the papers on the table and stared at Harold, sure he was up to something. Unable to figure out what, he turned on his heels and left. Dawson stood for a moment, not sure what to do, then hurried after him.

Harold walked with Traci to the front door and while pointing to different rooms and acting like he was describing what was in them, apologized for all the secrecy. After seeing Big G in action, he was sure she understood.

She thanked him for the information, hurried down the steps, and got in a cab waiting at the curb.

A few days after Harold met with the reporter, the limousine bringing Big G to work approached the front of the museum then sped away when protesters carrying signs ran down the steps, ready to deliver their complaint the moment he got out of the car. When they were safely around the corner, he called Dawson and told him to find out what was going on. He said they would circle the block and pick him up, but he had to be quick, they only had a second or two to pull it off.

As they approached the museum, Big G watched the protesters carry Dawson toward the dumpster behind the building. They drove to the closest Big G store where more protesters blocked the entrance to the parking lot, preventing customers from getting in.

Since he couldn't go to his office in the museum, he returned home and after getting settled in his study, opened the morning newspaper. The first thing he saw was a full color photograph of a Big G truck parked by a pond and the driver pouring something from a plastic container down a hole. ***Big G Grocery Caught Red Handed***," the headline announced in bold type. "While you were sleeping, Big G Grocery was polluting your drinking water. Where else are they dumping their putrid waste? Fleener Creek where you fish? Lake Meyer where you swim and water ski?" He saw the reporter who wrote the article was Traci Kline, the one he caught talking to Harold.

He'd suspected something was going on when he saw them together, now he had proof. He reached for the phone and was about to dial Harold's number and demand he leave the building immediately when he glanced at the other story on the front page. ***"Ambassador Given to Donate Famous Pen To The Otis Tharp Fountain Pen Museum."*** The article was also written by Traci Kline.

He put the phone on his desk and chewed his cigar, searching for a connection between the stories.

The fate of the *Community of Excellence* team forgotten; Clifford pushed through the dense undergrowth that covered what his father had identified as the *Mystery Trail*. He looked at the top of the trees, corrected his course, and plunged on. At one point it was so dark and the underbrush so thick, he feared for his life. In desperation he yanked a tangle of vines out of the way and stumbled into an open area. In the center of the space free of vegetation was a tree and, in the trunk of the tree, a door.

He opened it and entered a well-appointed room with a comfortable chair near a small window. On a table in a corner of the room was a letter addressed to him. With trembling paws, he opened it and found a note that read, *"I knew you'd find your way here. This is your place son, I built it for you."* It was signed Clifford and next to the name, to eliminate any legal challenge as to who owned the tree he'd added, *"Clifford's father."*

Clifford dropped the note on the table, overcome with emotion. Not just that his father left him this wonderful gift but without telling anyone, he'd found the end of the mystery trail. He sat down at the table, opened the pouch of maps he carried, and located the sheet with the list of trails yet to be discovered. He smiled with satisfaction as he drew a line through, *No. 3: Mystery Trail,* and wrote *"Found by Clifford,"* beside it. He didn't write Clifford's father because he figured everyone would know. "I'm young, he was old," he said quietly, "I don't see a problem."

HAPPY TRAILS TO YOU

Part 2: Keep Smiling Until Then

Few who meet bestselling author Leland Waffle realize they are witnessing the triumph of the human spirit over adversity. Or that, after observing him for years, social psychologists added another n to the age-old debate of nature or nurture, neglect.

Some found him socially awkward, difficult to talk to, and blunt to the point of being rude. Those who made it passed his gruff exterior, found a warm, caring person who would rush to their aid at the first sign of trouble and stay until a sense of normalcy returned.

Those who became friends, learned from an occasional offhand remark that he was raised on a country estate, isolated from other children. That his parents were seldom home, traveling to distant parts of the world for business or pleasure, leaving him in the care of cruel Nanny Gimlet. That he was home schooled by a series of tyrannical teachers who pushed him beyond what he was capable of achieving and ridiculed him mercilessly for a misplaced decimal point or misspelled word. And that, in the few moments he was alone, he wrote stories on scraps of paper about a world where parents loved their children and protected them from the dangers of the world.

In his teen years he was drawn to mysteries and, in his mid-twenties, created one of the most beloved characters in contemporary literature, Inspector BaGel. Those who study fiction know characters like the inspector are not made up out of thin air but drawn from people in the authors past. So the experts puzzled over, held seminars on, and wrote scholarly papers about who that character was. They would never have guessed it was a humble gardener named LeRoy, the one caring person who appeared briefly in Leland's life.

Walking passed a window, Nanny Gimlet looked out and saw Leland and LeRoy sitting together on a marble bench at the edge of a lush, well-tended garden. The next day she made him stand at the window and watch as LeRoy was escorted from the estate while repeating her warning that he should avoid contact with common laborers, they could not be trusted.

If there was a soft side to Inspector BaGel, if you're looking for a reason he only took cases others saw as hopeless or searched for an explanation for why he chose The Case Of The Missing Gardner *as the title of his first novel or wondered why he changed the inspector's name from Bagel to BaGel, look no further than LeRoy the gardener.*

A glimpse, however fleeting, of the authors background is helpful, especially when encountering his latest thriller, Friday the Inspector Turned In His Badge.

Roscoe put the book down after reading the introduction. He was relieved when JR told him it was polluted water from the pond, not squirrel fever that caused his illness. While the information was helpful, what he had was bad enough.

JR stopped by from time to time to tell him what was going on at the pond. Workers were using heavy equipment to scoop out the contents of the hole, then increased its size in case any of the noxious mixture had leeched into the ground around it. When they were satisfied, they'd reached the limits of the contamination, they filled the hole with clean dirt. Since the work started, regular testing by Ms. Rebecca and her students showed the quality of water was improving but not ready for community use.

After JR's latest visit, Roscoe reached for the Inspector BaGel book on the nightstand next to his bed. He couldn't remember when he'd had time to read without being interrupted by a community member facing a crisis or being called to an emergency meeting at the COC. He wondered if this was what life will be like when he retired. He dismissed the thought, writing it off as the lingering effect of an upset stomach.

After reading the introduction he turned to the dedication page. *"Look around. Can you find a truly honest person? Someone happy with who they are and the work they are doing? If so applaud them, for in a society clamoring for instant gratification, they will soon join the spotted owl on the list of endangered species."*

Puzzled by the dedication, he turned to the first chapter and began to read.

Inspector BaGel struggled to open his eyes. When he did, it made no difference, the area around him was as dark as when they were closed. He became aware of pain coming from a bump on his head. He reached to see if it was bleeding but couldn't move his arms and realized he was tied to a chair, his body restrained by ropes.

As he sat in the dark, he tried to remember how he got here.

It started when Commissioner Gleason called him to his office and told him what he was about to reveal was classified information, for the inspector's ears only. The Company, *who the inspector worked for, had known for some time an underground operation was delivering contaminated acorns to unsuspecting communities. The acorn cartel was rumored to be run by someone named Iago. Rumored because no one had been able to connect Iago Offshore Shipping Inc. and the illegal products entering the city.*

Until now.

A whistle blower had surfaced, offering to tell what he knew of the operation if he and his family were put in the witness protection program. The commissioner agreed, and a meeting arranged in an abandoned warehouse at midnight. The inspector was to go there, hear what he had to say, and confirm the information was worth the price The Company *paid for it.*

Two things about the assignment bothered the inspector. The first was, in his experience nothing good happened after midnight. The second, holding the meeting in a warehouse did not bode well for his safety. While it provided an isolated location, it also contained empty rooms, and discarded equipment, providing a hiding place for those the man was informing against. He would have mentioned this to the commissioner, but it would have done no good. He'd been told several times that dangerous situations were part of the job and, if he wasn't up to the task, someone was waiting to take his place.

The inspector entered the warehouse and waited in the shadows. It was a cloudy night so little natural light pierced the oil spattered windows. The bulb in the streetlight in front of the warehouse had burned out or been disabled, he had no way of knowing.

A door at the far end of the warehouse opened. It was followed by the sound of shuffling feet then a thud as whoever entered, fell to the concrete floor. Staying in the shadows, the inspector moved cautiously toward the prone figure. When he got there, he knelt beside him and after a quick inspection, determined from the wounds on his head and arms he'd received a terrible beating.

The victim's lips moved, and BaGel leaned closer to hear what he said. "Family... safe," he mumbled, and the inspector assumed he wanted to make sure the commissioner followed through on his promise to move his family to a different location with a new identity. "Your family will be taken care of. The commissioner will..." Before the inspector could finish, the man, although it caused a great deal of pain, shook his head, and mumbled so quietly the inspector strained to hear. "No commiss... Family safe, top shelf," were his last words. His eyes fluttered and his breathing, irregular when the inspector reached him stopped, leaving an unidentified body on the floor of an abandoned warehouse.

While trying to make sense of what he said, a door slammed at the back of the warehouse. Someone had been listening but what would they have heard? He was inches from the victim's mouth and could barely make out what he said. And why, knowing they would be his last words, did he shake his head at the mention of the commissioner's name? Finally, he wondered who the victim was and, if he wasn't talking about keeping his family safe, what he meant?

He knelt by the body, confronted by a problem that, at the moment, had more questions than answers.

Harold worked with a consultant to organize the presentation of the pen smuggled out of Galvonia. He usually worked alone and found it stimulating to kick ideas around with a creative person and develop what promised to be an impressive exhibit.

They considered having the dedication in the Grand Hall, a space large enough to accommodate the crowd they expected. They ruled it out because of the noise of the front door opening and closing and the high ceiling and hard surfaces creating echoes, making it difficult to hear. They thought of moving it to a room on the second floor but that would create a security nightmare for Officer Gardner.

They settled on the *Political Pens Room*, decided it was too large, and ran a partition across the middle, dividing the space in half. They moved everything out of the room, so all a visitor saw when he entered, was a wooden pedestal with the pen displayed in a box lined with red velvet. A single spotlight aimed at the pedestal highlighted the focal point of the display. On one wall was a map of the region with a star beside the name of the two countries. On the other was a picture of Galvonians celebrating what they thought was peace after years of fighting and disruption. Their joy was short lived when immediately after signing the treaty, the Gludistan army crossed the border and occupied the territory. The leaders of both countries dug in their heels and refused to negotiate.

To the right of the pedestal was a podium where Ambassador Given would stand when presenting the pen to the museum. When the ceremony was over, appetizers and soft drinks would be served in the Grand Hall. The flag of Galvonia would be located at one end of the serving table and its colors, chartreuse and blue, were reflected in the tablecloth and napkins.

Harold and the consultant were going over last-minute details when Dawson entered the room. He looked around, eventually focusing on the box on the walnut stand. He apologized for interrupting, said he was looking for Officer Gardner, and left. Harold was sure the moment the door closed he was on his way to Big G's office to report what he saw.

The night before the dedication, Harold walked around the room to make sure the changes he requested had been made. Satisfied he'd done everything he could to make sure the event received the attention it deserved, he closed the door and walked to his car.

After giving his report, leaving out the informers last words, Inspector BaGel waited as the commissioner walked to the window in his office and looked out, shaken by the news.

"He said nothing?" the commissioner asked.

Inspector BaGel shook his head.

The commissioner sighed, returned to his desk and said with frustration, "That was our only lead. I'm calling the investigation off, the case is closed, go back to what you were doing."

The inspector started to tell him there would be other informers, the wall of security around Iago was starting to crack. Before he could, the commissioner told him to, "Close the door on your way out, I have a call to make." The inspector was familiar with the move, it meant the subject was closed, the meeting over.

BaGel paced the floor of his office, disturbed by the commissioner's decision. To end an investigation that had been active for over a year because of one setback didn't make sense. The memory of the informant on the floor saying, "No commiss…" with his last breath had stayed with him.

Ignoring the commissioner's decision to stop the investigation, the inspector used his contacts in the department to identify who the informant was and where he'd lived. His house was in an older section of the city and, using the map function on his phone, found it.

He stood across the street from the abandoned house, looking for signs of life. He was dressed as a postman and carried a mailbag containing enough blank envelopes to appear genuine. He crossed the street and approached the house next to the informers. He pushed an envelope through the slot in the door, then walked down the sidewalk to the informer's house.

To someone driving by, it looked like a postman trying to figure out where to put the letter he was holding. He was going to knock but hesitated when he saw the door was partially open, never a good sign.

He stepped inside and called, "Hello?" several times but received no answer. He closed the door and waited, listening for a sound that would send him back to the street, but heard nothing. He walked down a narrow hallway, lit only by sunlight that pierced the tattered shades that covered dirty windows.

In a closet in the second bedroom, under a pile of discarded clothing, he found the safe. He looked up and saw, on the bottom of a shelf, a series of numbers he hoped was the combination. It was and, on the second try, *heard a click, and the door to the safe swung open. He didn't know what he expected to find but it certainly wasn't a map.*

A line was drawn from the Mexican border that ended with an arrow pointing at the city of Granville. Another line started in Canada and ended with its arrow touching the one from Mexico. The inspector looked closer and saw the arrows on the end of each line weren't just pointing at Granville, but at a place where the informant had written "City Hall." Next to it was, "Commissioner = Iago????"

The inspector wondered how much value to put on the work of an informer who would do anything to keep his family from danger. Could he have planted the material to throw suspicion on the commissioner, protecting the real culprit? If so, was it worth risking his life for? He heard footsteps behind him, and a muffled voice say, "Why couldn't you leave it alone?" The question was followed by a whoosh, as a club cut through the air and struck the back of his head, knocking him to the floor, unconscious.

The morning of the big event, Harold was about to enter the code on the keypad when the door of the security room opened, and Officer Gardner pulled him inside. Before closing the door, he looked in the hallway to make sure no one was watching. He told Harold he changed the code on the keypad because he was tired of Big G coming in before he got there, turning monitors on and off, and stinking up the place with his cigar.

"What is it? The new code?" Harold asked.

"My birthday, 9-4-82. I wanted something that was easy to remember." When he saw Harold looking for a piece of paper to write the number on he told him to memorize it, the way Big G roamed the halls at night, there was a chance he'd find it.

With that out of the way, he pointed to one of the monitors and said, "There's something you should see." He hit the enter key on the keyboard and sat back with a satisfied look on his face.

Harold found he was looking at the room created for the presentation of the pen. He started to say it looked the way it did when he was there last night when the door opened and quickly closed. Although the light was dim, when the intruder turned toward the display Harold recognized Dawson sent, he was sure, by his boss.

He tiptoed across the floor and lifted the pen from the display.

Officer Gardner stopped the action, looked at Harold and stuck a thumb in the air. They'd talked about the possibility of Big G sabotaging the event when the dedication of the pen was just an idea. They figured he'd do something to get even for Harold's role in the failed sales events, so they had a pen made of aluminum to look and feel like the one he'd received from the ambassador. The real pen was on the top shelf in Officer Gardner's locker.

Dawson took the pen in both hands and tried to break it in half. No luck. He raised it in the air and brought it down across his leg and, although there was no sound, his mouth flew open, and a look of pain shot across his face. In frustration he threw the pen on the floor and stomped on it.

When he was unable to destroy the pen, he stood for a moment, trying to decide what to do. The original plan called for him to break the pen in half and put both pieces in the box so when the ambassador picked it up, it would fall apart. Everyone would assume angry Gludistanians did it to let the world know they weren't happy with an event that raised sympathy for the Galvonian cause.

Since he couldn't break or bend the pen, he decided to take it, without it the ceremony would be a failure. He slipped it in his pocket and opened the door, planning to leave as quietly as he entered. He brought his hands to his ears and looked around in panic, the pen had activated the metal detector mounted in the door frame. He pulled the pen from his pocket, tossed it in the room, and closed the door.

Officer Gardner pointed to another monitor connected to the camera in the Grand Hall that showed Dawson limping up the steps to Big G's office.

They laughed and were about to smack hands when they heard the beep beep of someone operating the keypad outside the security room. The knob twisted but the door remained locked. When they couldn't get in, whoever it was tried again with the same result.

Frustrated, they kicked the door with their foot then walked away, grumbling.

Officer Gardner pointed to a monitor, and they watched Big G, chewing angrily on a cigar, climb the stairs to his office.

After regaining consciousness, Inspector BaGel determined he was tied to a chair in a room the size of a closet. He heard a groan and whispered, "Is someone there?"

A groggy voice answered, "Yes. I'm, ah..."

The inspector was relieved to find he wasn't alone. "Are you okay? Are you hurt?" He asked.

"I was... drugged. Something in my...walnut tea." The person hesitated, wondering if it was safe to reveal her identity. Then, deciding she had nothing to lose whispered, "I'm Agent Macintosh with the bureau."

"I'm Inspector BaGel with the Company," he said then wished he'd asked more questions to confirm the agent's identity before revealing who he was.

"Rita Macintosh," she said, wanting him to know he was talking to a female.

"Can you move Agent Macintosh? I'm tied to a chair."

"Same here but I think I can..." The inspector heard a grunt and the legs of a chair scrape the floor as she moved closer. "Keep talking. I'll come to you," she said, and the inspector started through what he knew of the case, ending with the informer and what he found at his house.

Soon she was next to him, and he felt a tug on the rope that held him to the chair. "I keep a small knife in my shoe," she said. The inspector felt the rope loosen, then he was free. He removed the rope that bound her and helped her to her feet. Soon they were moving their arms and legs, bringing circulation back.

Before they could compare notes, they heard voices outside the room they were in. He motioned for her to stand on one side of the door while he moved to the other. He tossed the end of the rope to her, and they pulled it taught a few inches above the floor.

They waited, afraid to speak for fear they'd be heard. It wasn't long before the door opened, and someone entered. They tripped over the rope and as they were falling, Rita brought a knee to his chin. The inspector heard a groan, then silence as the intruder fell to the floor.

They stepped out of the closet, planning to run to the exit but found the way blocked by Commissioner Gleason and Maxwell McGruder, the chief of police.

"There they are chief, caught red handed," the commissioner said as he stepped in the closet and removed a canvas bag. "I've had my eye on the inspector for some time and can say with certainty he is involved with the cartel." He lifted the bag and explained, "This is the payment he received for the last shipment."

Chief McGruder scratched his head, trying to make sense of what the commissioner said. He'd worked with the inspector on a few cases and although relentless in the pursuit of a suspect, he never crossed the line, doing something that would cause a judge to throw out the case before putting it on the docket. He mumbled, "Are you sure about this commissioner? I've known the inspec…"

"If you want to keep your job McGruder, arrest them." The commissioner was losing patience, he was also losing time. A new shipment of uninspected acorns was to be delivered to the warehouse and he had to be there to receive it.

"On what charge?" Officer McGruder asked.

"Smuggling acorns of questionable quality across the state line. Attempting to distribute said acorns to an unsuspecting public. Hiding the payment received for the acorns in a closet thus violating the Clean Building Act of 2013. Consorting with a federal agent to circumvent the law." He looked at Chief McGruder and asked, "How's that for starters?"

He glanced at his watch and told him, "Take them to the station and book them, I'm meeting with the mayor in ten minutes."

Chief McGruder followed him to the door and when he was sure he wasn't coming back asked, "What's going on BaGel? You smuggling acorns makes no sense."

Before the inspector could answer, Agent Macintosh said, "I have to check in with the bureau, they're probably wondering where I am." When she saw the concerned look on Chief McGruder's face she said, "I'll come to the station when I'm finished."

"Tell Agent Turnover hello for me, it's been a while since we've talked," the inspector said.

"I will," Rita said as she hurried out of the room.

"That may be a hard to do," the inspector told the chief after she'd gone, *"There's no one at the bureau named Turnover. I made it up, it's my favorite dessert."*

"But she said she would…" the chief looked at the door, then back at the inspector.

"She said a lot of things that aren't true. She didn't give her badge number so I doubt she could find the bureau, let alone identify the person in charge. And, if she was tied as tightly as I was, how did she manage to remove a knife from her shoe?"

"Do you think she'll come to the station like she said?" the chief asked, knowing the commissioner would be upset if she didn't.

"Not a chance but I know how to find her," the inspector said so casually the chief almost missed it.

"How could you possibly…" the chief stammered.

"While removing the rope releasing her from the chair, I put a tracking device in the pocket of her windbreaker." He opened his phone, tapped an app, and held it so McGruder could see a blinking light leave the building and start across the street.

"You need a court order to tamper…" the chief was a rule follower and knew, if they didn't go by the book, they'd be back at square one. It took a moment for him to realize the inspector had left the room and was halfway down the stairs.

Harold was pleased with the turnout for the dedication of the pen. Most came to hear what the ambassador had to say about the situation in Galvonia, the conflict was a popular subject on newscasts and talk shows. Others showed up because they'd been looking for a reason to come to the museum and the dedication was as good as any. The crowd filled the room the pen was in and overflowed into the Grand Hall where a large screen television located on the wall behind the sign-in desk displayed what was going on in the room. The original pen with the cap missing and teeth marks on one end, was put in the box and placed on the pedestal moments before the ceremony began.

At one o'clock Ambassador Given, after a brief introduction by Mayor Blanton, walked to the podium. He took his time getting there, shaking hands with the local businessmen who sponsored the event.

He put his prepared speech on the podium, slipped on his half glasses, and began. As he told the audience about the war in Galvonia, how he acquired the pen and Harold's part in organizing the event, Big G quietly opened the door and entered the room. He moved along the wall until he had an unobstructed view of the microphone the ambassador was holding. His plan was simple. Aim the remote control he was holding at the microphone, replacing what the ambassador said with the Gludistan national anthem. When the members of the GRM (Gludistan Resistance Movement) waiting in his office heard the music, they were to enter the room with weapons drawn and steal the pen.

Take that Squirrel Man Big G thought, referring to his suspicion that Harold was behind the two failed attempts to use the woods to promote his products.

When the ambassador finished his remarks and walked to the pedestal where the pen was displayed, Big G aimed the remote at the microphone and pressed play. Two things happened that weren't part of his plan. A woman standing near him saw the remote aimed at the ambassador and shouted, "Gun!" Within seconds federal agents, there to protect Ambassador Given, had Big G on the floor with his hands behind his back and his face in the carpet.

The other was, instead of the Gludistan anthem coming from the speaker, they heard a member of the resistance movement in Big G's office ask, "Is musik play yet?"

"Is musik play? There are no yet," another corrected him.

"Nyet?" a third said.

There was the sound of a door opening and the one who asked about the music said, "Good after the noon occifer, is this be grocery store?"

Harold stepped from the room in time to see Big G and his conspirators escorted down the front steps and into a van parked at the curb. As they were getting in, the spokesman for the resistance group asked Big G, "I am saying somethink wronk?"

Harold had invited Lloyd Brewster to the museum one afternoon when Big G was out of the office. He showed him the room for the ceremony and told him of his concern that Big G might do something to ruin the event. Lloyd studied the wiring diagram for the sound system and explained by switching a few connections in the control panel, he could reroute the signal from the microphone to Big G's office.

Rita was in a hurry. She hadn't expected the inspector to be thrown in the closet where she was hiding. Or the commissioner and chief of police to be waiting when the door opened.

If, on her way to the warehouse she'd shown a little caution and looked behind her, she would have seen the inspector and Chief McGruder jogging down the street, half a block away.

She entered the warehouse, waited for her eyes to adjust to the half-light, then with her back to an outside wall, slowly moved toward a solitary figure standing in the center of the room.

When she felt she was close enough, she left the shadows and approached the figure. She had to stall for time, the commissioner took the seeds she was going to use to pay for the shipment of illegal acorns.

"Don't know why, there are clouds in the sky," a male voice said the phrase that required a countersign from her, or the meeting was over.

"Stormy weather," she said as she moved closer. She gasped when instead Anton her normal supplier, she saw Commissioner Gleason.

"You blew it Rita," he said angrily. "What were you doing in the closet?"

"Where's Anton?" she asked, ignoring the question.

"I've eliminated the middleman; Anton is no longer part of the operation. From now on you'll deal directly with me." After saying it he thumped his chest with his paw.

"Eliminated?" Rita gasped, realizing if Anton was expendable, so was she.

"A figure of speech," the commissioner said. "Replaced. Removed." He waved a paw, mumbled, "Whatever," then "we've departed from the purpose of our meeting. The shipment of acorns has arrived, where are the seeds?"

He snapped his fingers, and an assistant dragged a bag of acorns across the floor and placed it near her feet.

"I don't have them with me. I left them in the..."

"Closet?" The commissioner said with a laugh as he lifted a canvas bag she recognized as the one that contained the payment for the shipment.

"Since you have the seeds, I'll take the..." she said as she reached for the bag.

"Not so fast," he said gruffly, and motioned for the assistant to grab her before she could get away.

"Put your hands in the air, we've heard enough," Inspector BaGel ordered as he stepped from behind a rusty piece of equipment and out in the open. "The police have surrounded the building, you won't get out of here alive."

"Who's going to take the word of a washed-up inspector against that of the leader of an agency tasked with protecting the community?" the commissioner said with a laugh.

"Me," Chief McGruder answered, holding a tape recorder in the air so the commissioner could see it.

"To the impartial observer, it will look like I broke the case wide open and captured the distributor. Rita Macintosh is Iago," the commissioner said loud enough for the recorder to pick up.

"That's not what I heard," Chief McGruder said and motioned for the patrolmen stationed at the door to arrest the commissioner and Rita.

As they were being led away Rita raised a paw, asking for a moment with the inspector. When they were alone, she took his paw in hers and said, "I felt something when we were in the closet like there was a chance for us. I have a few seeds tucked away, we could move to another city and start over."

Inspector BaGel had felt an attraction for her and could, by erasing the tape, remove the only solid piece of evidence against her and the commissioner. The other evidence they'd gathered was circumstantial, subject to interpretation "A lasting relationship is not built on dishonesty and ill-gotten gains," the inspector said and waved for the patrolman to take her away.

It was over. The ring smuggling acorns into the city was broken and its leader exposed. Why then, the inspector wondered, didn't he feel a sense of accomplishment? He guessed it was because he knew someone would fill the void left by Rita and Commissioner Gleason and the cycle of crime would continue, he'd seen it before.

Perhaps it is time to turn in my badge he thought, let someone younger take over who believes they can make a difference. With those thoughts swirling in his head, he opened the warehouse door and walked into the morning light, marking the start of a new day.

Roscoe put the book down and wished he'd read a little slower, but he felt compelled to keep going until he learned the fate of the inspector. He was sure being chairman of a small community couldn't match the fast-paced life of Inspector BaGel.

JR looked up from the book he was reading on geometrical shapes when Beck put her paws on his shoulders, leaned close and whispered, "So the rumor is false, you can read."

It took a moment for him to make the transition from what he was reading, to what she said. He shook his head and told her, "I just look at the pictures."

A library patron at a table near them cleared her throat and raised a paw to her lips, telling them to quiet down.

Beck giggled.

JR pointed outside.

They were holding paws when they walked by Webster, standing at the checkout desk. As they went by, he wondered how many happily joined couples in Abner started their life together in his library.

FIND THE NUT

Part 1: What Goes Around

Vincent "Vinny" Bling sat in the parking lot of the *Big G Grocery and Otis Tharp Fountain Pen Museum* waiting for a group of tourists to get on the bus they came in and leave. He could have had one of his, what do they call them now, associates do it. He didn't see anything wrong with gang member, it worked pretty well for his father. He didn't understand why everyone in the crime business was trying to be politically correct. You don't knock off a bank anymore, you make an unauthorized withdrawal. And you don't shove a note written on the back of an envelope to a teller demanding all the cash in the drawer, you give her a document written on a word processor that's been checked for spelling and punctuation errors.

But he reluctantly admitted, they were the new crop of gangster and the best thing for him to do was to go with the flow. Most had college degrees and were intent on changing the way things were done in the underworld. Tonight, while he was sitting in an empty parking lot, they were at some high dollar fundraiser to build an addition to the *Centerline Hospital for the Indigent and Infirm*.

And, while he was thinking about it, what happened to pinstriped suits and fedoras? The new guys walk around in pre-washed jeans with rips in the knees and their shirttail hanging out. Where do you keep a gun in an outfit like that? And, instead of wingtip shoes, they wear loafers with no socks.

He didn't get it. He started on the streets and worked his way up a very long ladder to become boss. No. Wait. He wasn't a boss he was a CEO. Or COO. Whatever.

He shrugged it off, it was time to go to work. He left his car, walked across the field and entered the woods. With the help of a flashlight, he followed the path he'd taken days before. That was another thing that bugged him, you don't use payphones to set up a bank heist anymore, you tweeted, or sent a text message, leaving a trail a federal agent with half a brain could follow.

He found the place he was looking for, removed leaves covering the hole he'd dug earlier and dropped a bundle of one-hundred-dollar bills wrapped in cellophane in it. He pushed dirt back in the hole with his foot, smoothed the surface with his hand, then slid a patch of sod back in place.

He let the beam of the flashlight play over the ground and decided if you didn't know where to look, you wouldn't notice the difference between his "project" and the area around it. The new guys can have their offshore accounts and fancy spread sheets, he'll take a hole in the ground every time. You're the only one who knows where it is, so there's no one to spill the beans when questioned by the cops. And there's no combination to remember to open a locker at the train station.

That's what his father Vincent "Vinny" Bling Sr. taught him. "Stick youse cash in de ground and when youse needs it, it's waitin there, safe and sound. They check youse bank accountings and investment portfolics, but never look below ground." After saying it he would tap the floor of his condominium with the toe of his shoe.

This was the fourth bundle he'd buried in different parts of the woods over the last few months and at the rate things were going, in a year, maybe two, he'd dig them up, leave the nine to five, which for him was nine at night to five in the morning, rat race and have some fun. Maybe take a cruise to an exotic island and not come back.

He followed the path to the parking lot, got in his car, and drove away.

Leon woke up in time to see a human leave the woods and cross the field to Seed Man's building. He guessed he'd dozed off, he didn't remember seeing him enter. The problem facing him was should he report it to Lothar. If he did, he'd become Exhibit A for what happens when you fall asleep on the job and allow humans to traipse around the woods unnoticed. There was no one around so if he didn't record it who would know? He decided to keep his mouth shut and his eyes open until his shift was over.

Roscoe looked up when the door to the meeting room opened and Darin entered. He glanced at his planner to see if he was here for a meeting. He was about to ask the reason for the visit when Darin pulled an envelope from the mailbag that hung from his shoulder and slid it across his desk.

Roscoe started to say he didn't have to deliver it personally, but Darin stopped him with, "It's a registered letter." He put a form next to the envelope, pointed to a place at the bottom and said, "You have to sign so they know you received it."

Roscoe was about to sign the form when Chet, feature writer for the *Abner Echo,* strolled in and asked if Roscoe had seen his notepad. He had it at last night's committee meeting but when he got to his office this morning, he couldn't find it. He walked to the conference table, checked to make sure they weren't looking, tossed the notepad under the table, dropped to one knee and shouted, "Found it."

Two committee members entered. They'd seen Darin and Chet come in and wondered if Roscoe had called an emergency meeting and failed to invite them.

Roscoe thanked Darin for delivering the letter, pushed it aside, and picked up the report he was reading before he came in.

When Darin didn't leave, Chet moved closer to Roscoe's desk. The committee members changed position to get a better look at the letter.

Roscoe realized they weren't going to leave until he opened it, so he put the report on his desk, and picked up the letter.

"Did I mention it's registered?" Darin asked and pointed at the envelope in case Roscoe missed, **URGENT! OPEN IMMEDIATELY!** stamped on the back.

"It's from the Committee of Committees," Chet said when he saw the COC stamp on both sides of the envelope. He wrote, "Letter from COC arrived..." in his notepad and looked for a calendar. When he didn't see one, he added, "today." He waited with the point of his pencil pressed against a page of his notepad, ready to record what was in the envelope.

Roscoe pulled a letter opener from the drawer and slid it beneath a flap, held in place by a wax seal. He removed the letter, opened it and read so all could hear, "Congratulations. The Community of Abner has been selected to host the first of what we hope will become an annual event, the *All Neighborhood Find The Nut Competition*. Six teams have signed up so far. We expect twice that many when the tournament begins. Your community was chosen because of its reputation for consistently exceeding expectations on projects in the past. We are confident the same high standard will produce a tournament other communities will strive to duplicate."

It was signed by Leander, secretary to the highly exalted chairman. There was a note beneath his signature that said, "Sorry for the short notice. I am sending Casey, an event planner we've used in the past to help. Teams will arrive later this week"

Roscoe dropped the letter on his desk and put his head in his paws. He couldn't keep up with things now, where would he find time to organize a find the nut tournament?

Chet turned the letter so he could copy the information word for word.

Darin picked up the form Roscoe signed and left.

The committee members followed him, content in the knowledge they would be the first to tell those in the Clearing what was going on. The other reason for leaving was, if they hung around any longer, they'd end up in charge of something.

Mo, short for Moses, is passionate about the sport of find the nut. He owns a shop that sells find the nut paraphernalia; sashes worn by the players, spades for the diggers, and protective eyewear for defenders. His love for the sport started when he was a first year in seed school and didn't make the team. Rather than sulk over the setback, he volunteered to be a manager. Coach Bobby was just starting a string of undefeated seasons and liked his attitude. He took him under his wing and during the three years they were together, taught him everything he knew about the sport.

Mo went from equipment manager, to trainer, to assistant coach while in school and, after graduating, opened the first of what he hoped would become a chain of *Play Mo Sports* stores. Having Coach Bobby's name on his resume opened doors that were closed to others. He was able to make ends meet financially by preparing fields for league play and hiding the nut, a skill he perfected while in seed school. Bury it too deep and the diggers can't find it, too shallow and the game was over before the spectators were settled in the stands.

One afternoon while getting a field ready for a competition, he had an idea that would transform his business and connect his name with famous players in the sport. The idea that took a number of false starts to perfect, was the *Mo Nut Placer*, a tube, sharpened on one end with marks on the side to let the user know when they reached the proper depth. When a nut was dropped in the tube it came to rest at the perfect location. The only problem was when the tube was removed it left a small mound of dirt, something a skilled player would notice immediately. Tamping it down with his foot would be a dead giveaway that something was there.

That's when he had his second idea; insert the tube at an angle. It sounds simple when you hear it but it took a huge leap of imagination to cross the boundary between his device and the way things were done. He changed the shape of the tube, adjusted the marks on the side, and the first time he used it he knew he had a winner. Going in at an angle allowed him to start several feet from where the nut would end up. And, coming in from the side instead of straight down, didn't leave a mark when the tube was removed.

He changed the name to the *Mo Angled Placer* and over time, shortened it to *MAP*.

He had no way of knowing as he climbed the stairs to the meeting room to volunteer to prepare the field for the *All Neighborhood Find the Nut Tournament*, his life and the lives of those coming to the tournament would be changed, and not in a good way.

Roscoe looked up when he heard a *thump* from something dropped on the platform outside the meeting room, and an exasperated voice say, "Unbelievable!"

He was halfway out of his chair when the door opened and a short, stocky female carrying a suitcase, entered. "How is a person supposed to find this place? There are no signs. No distinguishing landmarks. Nothing that says welcome to Abner. Nada. Zilch." She walked around the room muttering, "I'm good but I'm not a miracle worker and that's what it's going to take to pull this shindig off, a miracle." She approached Roscoe's desk, shook her head, and said in disgust, "And you've done nothing about it."

Roscoe was stumped. They hadn't met, yet she was walking around like she owned the place. He was astonished by her in your face attitude, so any effort on his part to be civil was thrown out the window when he asked, "Who are you?"

"Who am I?" she said then shook her head. "Why am I not surprised? How do you get your mail? Carrier pigeon? Smoke signals? Drums?"

"Of course not. We have a first rate..."

"So, you're saying the COC dropped the ball? That's a shocker." She looked at Roscoe, shook her head and said, "Leander tells me to pack my bag and hightail it out here and I waste valuable time wandering around in the woods because THERE ARE NO SIGNS!" The last words were accompanied by the sound of her fist pounding on his desk.

The mention of Leander's name caused something to click in Roscoe's mind. "The COC sent you? To Abner?"

"Why else would I come to this, what do you call yourselves, a community wannabe? A mini com? You're not just out of the way, you're way out of the way."

"You must be..." Roscoe almost had it. Several days had passed since he received Leander's letter, but he was expecting a...

"Casey, with a C," she said and stuck out a paw. "The clock's ticking Mr. Chairman. We have less than a week to pull off this boondoggle and I'm standing in a room not large enough to hold the paper cups needed to hold drinks for thirsty spectators." She shook her head, overwhelmed by the task facing her.

"Could we start over. I think we..." Roscoe said, extending a paw.

"That's a great idea Mr. Chairman," she shot back. "Let's kick back, have some walnut tea, and shoot the breeze about the good old days." She put her paws on his desk, leaned toward him and said in a voice loud enough to be heard in the Clearing, "THERE. IS. NO. TIME."

"I just thought..."

"I had a month to prepare for celebrating the twentieth anniversary of the Committee of Committee's. Three weeks for the installation of Cletus as the highly exalted chairman, and three days for this... find the nut thing. That's my reward for producing under pressure, more pressure and an impossible deadline," she muttered as she paced around the room, punching the air with her fists.

"Welcome to Abner," Roscoe said.

His greeting took her by surprise. No apology for lack of signage. Nothing to indicate he'd thought about the tournament since receiving the letter.

He left his desk, opened the door, and said, "Let me show you around."

As they walked through the Clearing, Roscoe introduced her to those gathered there. "This is Casey. She's an event planner from the COC." They nodded like they knew what an event planner was.

He took her to the safety training room because he was sure first aid would be required during the tournament. They talked as they walked the path to the playing field, and it became obvious to Roscoe she knew nothing about the game of find the nut, she hadn't played or attended a match. He told her he'd arrange for Coach Bobby, recently inducted into the Find the Nut Coaches Hall of Fame, retired and living at the Senior Center, to explain the fundamentals of the game. When they reached seed school he said if she needed more than a corner of the meeting room to store things, she could use the gymnasium. Or the auditorium. "Let Principal Charles know what you need, he's expecting to hear from you."

He told her Mo was getting the field ready, gave her a list of volunteers to sell refreshments and take tickets, and said if she needed anything she knew where to find him. As he walked away, he heard, "Mister chairman. I'm sorry if I..."

He raised a paw and told her, "Don't worry about it."

Mo felt something was needed to let those attending the tournament know this was not an ordinary find the nut competition, it was the All-Neighborhood Championship. His idea, like most in situations like this, started off complicated and moved to simplicity. He thought of working the names of the competing teams into a logo in the middle of the field, but new ones were added daily. Several withdrew when they found teams from larger communities were coming and knew they didn't have a chance of winning.

Eventually he settled on two circles, one inside the other. He filled the center one with red chalk, and hoped the crowd got that it represented the passion players have for the sport. The outer circle was white and stood for unity.

When he finished, he felt that was as good as he could do in the time he was given. He left the field to get his equipment bag, all that remained was hiding the nut.

When he returned, he found a human, on his hands and knees looking at the design he'd made.

"Toby? Ryan here," the human said into something he held to his ear, "You won't believe what I found. It's fabulous," Mo didn't understand human sounds but caught the excitement in his voice. "It's not from this world, that's for sure. It's like crop circles on a smaller scale." The human aimed his phone at the symbol, took a picture and asked, "Got it?" He waited until the listener received the picture then said, "I've marked the spot with my GPS and going back to the office for lights and a high-definition camera."

He studied the symbol and wondered what would have happened if he'd stayed in his cubicle instead of going for a walk in the woods to clear his head. He smiled at his good fortune as he left to get the equipment required to take a better picture.

Mo waited until he was gone before looking for a place to bury the nut. Normally he found a spot in the shade of a tree or near a group of rocks, someplace the players wouldn't expect. He found the perfect location in a corner of the field surrounded by tall grass. If the attackers weren't paying attention, they'd run by without seeing it.

He lifted the nut from its case, pushed the *MAP* under the leaves, but stopped when he bumped into something solid. He removed a patch of sod, pushed the dirt aside, and saw a bundle of green paper wrapped in a clear material.

He backed away from the hole and tried to think of what to do.

When he got to the meeting room, he knocked on the door. The sergeant of arms opened it and told him Roscoe was in a meeting and couldn't be disturbed. He walked across the platform and sat down on the top step. After sitting for a moment, he shook his head and said, "This is important. It can't wait." He knew if he knocked again, he'd be stopped by the sergeant at arms and be back where he started. He got up and walked around the tree the meeting room is in, looking for a way to contact Roscoe. He stopped when he saw the small window, reached in his equipment bag, removed a piece of chalk, climbed the tree, and wrote, "HELP!" in large letters on the glass.

He climbed down and was putting the chalk back in the bag when the door to the meeting room opened, and the sergeant of arms hurried toward him. He had a, did you think I was kidding when I told you Roscoe was busy, look on his face. He was about to make him climb up and clean the window when Roscoe asked, "What's going on?"

If it had only been Roscoe, Mo would have been okay. But faced with the committee, an angry secretary, and a sergeant at arms twice his size, he couldn't remember why he was there or what he'd written on the window.

He shook his head, lifted his paws and said, "Mr. Chairman, we have a problem."

Vinny waited in his car until the lights in the museum went out and the cleaning crew got in their cars and left the parking lot. He'd gone through the money he'd hidden faster than he thought possible.

The downturn in the economy had slowed his income stream to a trickle. Petty theft was hardly worth the effort because people were selling their possessions to make ends meet. Stealing credit cards was a waste of time, most had reached their limit or been canceled. Couple that with the price of bribing city officials going up and he was hurting financially.

To make matters worse, he'd received word from a confidential source, he was being audited by the IRS for claiming members of his gang as dependents on his income tax form.

When he reached the edge of the woods, he turned on his flashlight and followed the path to the hole containing the last bundle of money. There was enough for him to leave Centerline and lay low until the investigation was over.

He found the hiding place, pushed the piece of sod away, reached down, and found... a nut.

At the same moment he discovered the money was gone, a portable generator started, and a row of temporary lights came on. Ryan, with two fingers of his right hand forming a V, stepped out of the shadows, pointed to the acorn Vinny was holding and asked, "Is that how you communicate with," he pointed to the sky, "them?"

Vinny shaded his eyes with his hand and looked around, trying to figure out what was going on. It was the middle of the night, and the place was lit up like it was noon. He shrugged and said, "Nah. It's a nut." He stood, said, "Well, I'm taking off," and started to leave, wondering if he'd been set up by a rival gang who'd heard he was having financial problems and felt it was time to move in.

"I come in peace," Ryan said and, realizing he'd caught the visitor by surprise added, "Don't go until you tell us what it means."

"Us?" Vinny stammered. "It?" he added as he backed away, thinking the stranger was talking about the hole in the ground.

"The marking in the field," Ryan said, pointing over his shoulder.

Vinny had no idea what the guy was talking about.

"Are they religious in nature? Celestial? Do they contain a message? A warning?" Ryan asked, anxious for answers.

Vinny had been in difficult situations before. He walked the line between law enforcement breathing down his neck and gangs from out of town trying to take over his territory, so he wasn't completely helpless. Once he overcame the shock of not finding the money and his eyes adjusted to the light, he was thinking more clearly. The guy with the ponytail said something about markings in a field. "Yeah, sure," he told him, "one of them."

"Which?" Ryan pressed for more information.

Vinny walked over, grabbed the front of Ryan's sweater and growled, "It's a warning, okay? Don't take stuff that ain't yours."

Ryan stammered, "You're not from?" He struggled, trying to find a word to describe something as vast as the universe, "Out there?" he said feebly, pointing to the sky.

"Nah," Vinny grunted and nodded in the direction of downtown Centerline, "Over there."

"Our technicians ran a digital image of the marking through our computer and found no connection between it and political events. There have been no recent UFO sightings or significant change in global temperature so until tonight, we didn't know who made them."

"Show me what you got," Vinny said and when Ryan started toward the markings, he took off in the opposite direction.

"My research of mysterious symbols suggests..." When Ryan reached the circles Mo made, he turned and discovered Vinny had gone as mysteriously as he appeared.

Roscoe and Mo watched the scene from beneath the temporary bleachers set up for the tournament. After the humans left Roscoe asked, "What do you think?"

Mo shrugged. "If he doesn't take the lights, the championship game could be played at night."

Unfortunately, the tournament didn't last long enough for a final game. The first match ended in a draw because neither team found the nut. They demanded Mo show them where it was buried or they'd file a protest with FTNA, the *Find the Nut Association*. He left the bleachers, walked to the spot where he put the nut, removed the sod, and found the hole was empty. "I don't understand, I put it here yesterday," he moaned but couldn't be heard over the shouts of angry players demanding their entrance fee back.

Roscoe looked up when the door to the meeting room opened and Casey entered. She walked to his desk, looked him in the eye and said, "If this" she searched for a word, "disaster shows up on my record, I'm coming back to Abner and knock heads. Do I make myself clear?"

Roscoe raised his paws and told her, "They'll hear nothing from me."

After a commercial break Linda Bogart, anchor person for the evening news, told the viewers they were going to the parking lot of the *Big G Grocery and Otis Tharp Fountain Pen Museum* for a late breaking story from action reporter Flo Billings.

Flo waited for the cameraman to point to her before saying, "Tonight, in a wooded area in the heart of the city, an unusual meeting took place." She turned to the person standing next to her. "I'm talking to Ryan Bishop, a..."

"Symbolist," Ryan provided the word she was looking for then added, "not cymbalist," sharing an inside joke familiar to those in his field of study.

Flo didn't get it. She tilted the microphone toward him and said, "Tell us about your," she made quote marks with her fingers, "close encounter."

"Okay. So, like he appeared out of nowhere. While walking in the woods I found a symbol on the ground. I was going to photograph it but when the lights came on, he was on his hands and knees meditating or drawing another symbol." He opened the photo album in his phone, found what he was looking for, and turned it so the viewers could see. It showed a man in a pinstriped suit on his hands and knees, shielding his eyes from the light. His hat had fallen to the ground, revealing a shiny bald head, and gold earring.

"And you think he's an alien?" She asked, skeptically.

"From space? Yes, I do. I asked where he was from and he said over there," Ryan pointed to the horizon.

Flo looked where he was pointing and asked, "A star? A solar system?"

Ryan ignored the sarcasm in her question, he was used to it. "He said he made the symbol to send a message."

"And the message is?"

"Don't mess with my stuff." Ryan realized that wasn't exactly right, so he changed it to, "Don't take stuff that ain't yours."

"Stuff?" Flo asked, confused.

"I think he was saying we should stick to things on earth and leave space alone. I mean look at the mess we've made of our planet. Global warming. Polar ice caps melting. What will happen when we build colonies out there? More congestion? More pollution? More..."

Flo brought the microphone close to her mouth and said in a whisper, "A visitor from space arrived in Centerline last night with a message for all humanity, don't take stuff that ain't yours. Is that right Ryan?"

"It is. And while I have the opportunity, I would like to point out that lack of funding for deep space research is destroying any chance we have of..." Ryan was still talking when Flow turned to the camera and said, "Back to you Linda."

Harold walked across the parking lot and went through his taking the squirrels home in his car routine. He opened the trunk, removed a bundle of newspapers, and carried them to the dumpster. While tossing it in, he heard movement behind him. It wasn't unusual for several squirrels to jump in when the trunk was open. He returned to his car, closed the trunk, and drove away.

If he'd been paying attention instead of thinking about the odd conclusion at the dedication of the pen that afternoon, he would have noticed a late model car with the headlights off, follow him out of the parking lot.

When he pulled in his garage, he repeated what he did at the dumpster. He opened the trunk, and to kill time, moved paint cans from one side of a shelf to the other. When enough time passed for his passengers to get out, he returned to close the trunk lid and saw a grocery bag behind the spare tire. Curious, he looked inside and saw bundles of one-hundred-dollar bills wrapped in cellophane.

He closed the trunk, put down the garage door, and slowly climbed the steps to the kitchen. He had some thinking to do.

FIND THE NUT

Part 2: Comes around

Harold couldn't sleep. When he closed his eyes, he saw the sack of money in the trunk of his car. He wished he'd looked when he heard movement at the dumpster, but if he had, what would he have seen? Big G's managers setting him up, claiming he stole it from the grocery store in the museum? Was it a robbery gone bad? The thief needed a place to hide the loot and the open trunk looked like the perfect place. The most frightening thought was, would whoever put it there be waiting for him when he got to work in the morning?

Thoughts bounced from one side of his brain to the other until, around midnight, he moved to the recliner in the family room, usually a sure-fire answer for sleep problems. This time changing locations couldn't turn off the churning thoughts that never ended well. He was relieved when the sky began to lighten, and the newspaper slammed against the front door.

While getting ready for work he decided to follow his normal routine only instead of carrying newspapers to the dumpster, he'd take the sack of money. It may not make it back to the rightful owner, but it would no longer be his problem.

Thelma was still sleeping when, after a quick shower and dressing in the dark, he went down the steps to the garage. He pressed the opener and while the door was going up, he moved to the back of the car to look in the trunk to see if the money was actually there or if it was the product of an overactive imagination. He stopped halfway to the door when he saw a man in a pinstriped suit and wearing a fedora, leaning against the hood of a late model car, parked in a way that blocked any chance he had of leaving the garage.

"Wha..." was all he could say before the stranger pushed off the car, flipped the toothpick he'd been chewing in the grass near the

98

driveway and said, "I'm Vinny Bling and youse has something that belongs to me." He pointed to the trunk and added, "In there."

"Something of yours? In the..." Harold stammered, having trouble getting his thoughts together.

"When I couldn't find what I was looking for in the woods, I had my associate Bruno keep an eye on the parking lot. He saw youse take something out of the dumpster and put it in the trunk of youse car."

"He was mistaken. It was dark..." Harold decided he wouldn't mention there was the possibility the squirrels put it there unless he had to.

"Hey, we could stand here busting our chops doing the I said youse said routine, but I got better things to do with my time. So, what do youse say youse opens the trunk and we takes a look-see. If I find youse has what I'm looking for I'll take it and go. If not," he shrugged, "Bruno got it wrong."

Harold had hoped it wouldn't come to this. That some act of nature would prevent him from opening the trunk. A random lightning strike or spontaneous microburst. When neither occurred, he pressed the button on the key that opened the trunk, closed his eyes, and waited for the worst.

Vinny looked, shrugged, said, "So, Bruno got it wrong," walked to his car, opened the door, and got in.

"I worked out a routine with the... I'm sorry, what?" Harold said, giddy with relief.

"If youse should find a bag of cash in or around the dumpster, I can be found at *Rosie's Pizza and Pub* every day at noon."

While Vinny was getting in his car, someone on the sidewalk hollered, "It's him. The alien I saw on the ten o'clock news." A crowd quickly formed, and her comment was followed by, "What's he doing here?" "Did he make a symbol in Harold's backyard?" "Can aliens drive cars?"

Myron Boggs pushed through the crowd and hurried down the driveway, waving a copy of the home's association bylaws. "Harold," he called, "there are rules about leaving a car in the driveway overnight."

Vinny backed up the driveway and the crowd scattered when their effort to get his autograph failed to slow him down. Myron dove out of the way to keep from being hit. He took a moment to straighten his clothes then walked briskly to Harold who greeted him with a hug and a heartfelt, "Thank you."

An act of nature had occurred in the form of Myron Boggs his trouble making neighbor.

Myron is uncomfortable with displays of affection, preferring to wave or nod instead of shaking hands. While getting himself together, Harold looked in the trunk of his car and, other than the bundle of newspapers he put there last night, the money was gone.

It didn't make sense. The trunk was locked, the garage door closed, and the security system activated. Yet the sack there last night, was gone this morning.

Harold parked in his reserved place, walked to the rear entrance of the museum, entered the code on the keypad, but the door didn't open. He tried again, thinking he must have switched numbers the first time but got the same results. There was no click, letting him know the door had unlocked, only a mechanical voice telling him, "The number you entered is incorrect. Please try again." He tried the doorknob, but it wouldn't turn. He guessed it was out of order and Officer Gardner hadn't had time to fix it. On his way to the front of the building he walked by Dawson's car, glanced in the back seat, and saw part of a sign with **Vote**, the name of the candidate was covered by a stack of campaign literature, **For Mayor**. He was surprised to find Dawson had a life away from Big G Grocery, apparently, he dabbled in politics.

After going through the front entrance and up the wide stairway to the Grand Hall, he was met by Officer Gardner who apologized for the inconvenience before saying, "Sorry but I have to look in your briefcase."

He asked why, got a shrug and a mumbled, "Big G's orders." Officer Gardner closed the briefcase and asked if he had a mobile phone. Harold was going to remind him he knew he had one because he borrowed it once when the battery in his died. He nodded and Officer Gardner pointed to a box with a handwritten sign above it that said *Cell Phones Here*.

As he was walking to his office in the security room Officer Gardner told him, "There's a meeting in Big G's office. He took everyone's phone, he doesn't want anyone recording it."

"When?" Harold asked, he needed to make a phone call before the meeting started. Officer Gardner glanced at the large clock above the entrance with the hour and minute hands made of fountain pens and said, "Now."

Harold was the last to enter. Big G motioned for Officer Gardner to close the door and not let anyone near his office. He'd heard there were microphones that could pick up conversations through doors and windows.

After taking a moment to survey the group he said, "I've increased the level of security because I don't want what I am about to tell you to get out before I make the announcement. Is that understood?"

"You can count on us." "Absolutely." "Our lips are sealed." From the managers.

Harold didn't reply. He wasn't actually part of the Big G management team, but as curator of the museum he knew where things in the building were located others didn't.

Big G walked to the window, took the stub of a cigar from his mouth, and using it as a pointer asked, "What do you see out there?"

"A parking lot." "The woods." "The top of the buildings downtown." From the managers.

Big G stuck the cigar back in his mouth and bit down to keep from unloading on them for their inability to see what was obvious to him. He took a deep breath, let it out and said, "I see a city crying for leadership."

The managers nodded, letting him know that's what they saw.

"The citizens of this great city are looking for someone tested by the fire of competition. A graduate of the school of hard knocks. A leader who can hold his own in the rough and tumble of today's business environment. Someone who rose above the small minded critics, anxious to sling mud on a record of continued success." He paused and gave them a moment to think about what he said before asking, "Who do you know with those qualifications?"

The managers looked at each other, hoping one of them would come up with a name and get them off the hook.

Big G tilted his head to one side. Dawson stepped forward and, after clearing his throat to get their attention said, "Those are pretty big shoes to fill sir. You're the only one I know who can do it."

"Of course." "You have our vote." "How can we help?" The managers said, anxious to get back on his good side.

"Thoughts Finebender?" Big G asked and the managers stepped aside, opening a space between the two men.

"About?" Harold asked, not sure what he was supposed to say.

"Me. Stepping into the breech. Throwing my hat in the ring," from Big G.

"Your hat?" Harold knew what he wanted but wasn't about to give him the satisfaction of saying it.

Big G put his hands on his desk, leaned toward Harold and said like a teacher talking to a simple-minded student, "Me. Running for mayor. Stepping into the nitty-gritty and getting the city back on the straight and narrow."

"Mayor Blanton is..." Harold stopped when Big G slammed a fist on his desk and bellowed, "Mayor Blanton is like a duck in a new world. He couldn't put groceries in a sack if the instructions were written on the side." Big G threw the cigar at the wastebasket, missed, and two of the managers dove for it. One got it and put it in his pocket, not wanting anything to keep him from hearing the exchange between the two men.

"His position on the minimum wage is..." Harold was prepared to defend someone he considered a friend. Before he could finish Big G fumed, "Putting people like me out of business. Workers earning a minimum wage should feel lucky they have a job. If they kept their nose to the grindstone and did what they were told they wouldn't have time to gripe about how little they're paid. When my father got in the grocery business, he didn't have two nickels to rub together.

If the truckload of watermelons hadn't..." He stopped, not wanting to go there. He waved a hand, letting Harold know the discussion was over.

"If I could say..." Harold wanted the managers to know Big G had distorted the mayor's position on the minimum wage issue.

"We've moved on Finebender, try to keep up," Big G growled as he lifted a poster from his desk advertising a rally in the field behind the museum. As he was going over the details, explaining that was where he would announce he was running for mayor, Harold studied the poster. The field was filled with people. It looked like a section of the woods had been cleared to make room for a platform where Big G and those backing his bid for mayor would stand.

Big G explained the role the managers would play in getting him elected and wrapped it up by saying, "Running for office is like selling groceries. Wrap moldy lettuce in shiny paper, stick a label on it that says the price is reduced by twenty percent and customers will stand in line to buy it."

"Excuse me, but is the speaker's platform in the woods?" Harold asked, pointing at the poster.

Big G lifted a scrap of paper the size of the platform from his desk, held it on the poster with a pudgy finger and said, "If I put it in the field, I'll lose, what do you think guys, twenty or thirty supporters?"

"Easily." "Absolutely." "Maybe more." From the managers.

"The woods belong to the city. You can't..." He stopped when Big G waved his hands and said, "Someone goes there at night, cuts down the trees, and in the morning, I report an act of vandalism occurred behind my building. It happens all the time."

"Are you telling us to cut down the trees without getting a permit from the city?" Harold couldn't believe he'd suggest something like that.

Big G raised his bushy eyebrows and opened his hands, wondering where a thought like that came from. "I was simply providing a possible scenario in response to your question about how it could be done." He looked at the managers, "Did I tell you to cut down the trees?"

"No sir." "Not that I heard." "You would never ask us to do that." They answered, outraged that Harold would suggest such a thing.

Harold was about to suggest it would be easier to build a temporary platform in the parking lot when Big G's secretary stepped in the office and handed him a slip of paper. He glanced at it and said, "Excuse me, I have to take this call." As he was leaving Big G said, "Let me know your game plan for building the platform, you don't have much time."

Harold hurried to his office, tapped the code into the keypad, went to his desk and dialed the number on the note the secretary gave him. A receptionist thanked him for calling the First Bank of Centerline and asked how she could be of service. He told her who he was and was going to explain he was returning a call but before he could finish, she said, "I'll transfer you to Mr. Tracy's office."

"Mr. Tracy?" he repeated and wondered why the president of the bank would be calling him. Mr. Tracy glanced at the caller ID, whispered, "It's him," and handed the phone to someone.

"Harold?" Thelma said through tears, "How could you?"

"Sweetheart, are you okay? Did something happened at the bank?" he asked, concerned.

"Get down here immediately and straighten this out," she said through clenched teeth. "If you don't, they're taking me to jail and booking me for money laundering."

Harold looked at the phone, puzzled by what she said. They didn't keep more than a few dollars in the house for an emergency, if they purchased something they used credit cards.

He wrote a note saying he'd gone to handle a family emergency, put it on Officer Gardner's desk, opened the door, and bumped into Dawson holding a box of office supplies. "Thanks for getting the door," he said, a little out of breath.

"What's going on?" Harold asked, glanced at his watch and saw he was losing time.

"Big G told me to move in with you since we're working on the platform project together." He pointed over his shoulder, "There's another box. If you'll get it, I'll hold the door so you won't have to..."

"Maybe later," Harold told him as he hurried to the back door.

Mr. Tracy's secretary ushered him into his office. He saw Thelma wagging a finger in the bank president's face, threatening to sue him for every penny he had. When she saw Harold, she put her hands on her hips, glared at him, and said, "It took you long enough to get here."

Mr. Tracy felt the tension between them and said he'd step outside so they could talk things over in private. The door was the only one way in or out of his office. An alarm would go off if she tried to open a window, there was no way for her to escape. He told Harold he was sure there was an explanation for what happened and hoped this wouldn't damage the good relationship the bank had with the museum.

After he left, Harold asked his wife, "What's going on?"

She started to say something sarcastic then, overcome by the events of the morning, sat down in a chair, dabbed her eyes with a handkerchief and groaned, "I've never been so humiliated in my life. Escorted through the lobby by a security guard like a common criminal. What if someone from our neighborhood saw me? Or a member *of Women Who Wear Gray Shoes?*"

Harold sat in the chair across from her, took her hands in his and said, "Start at the beginning and don't leave anything out."

She took a deep breath, let it out, and explained when it took longer than usual for him to come to the kitchen last night, she went halfway down the basement stairs and saw him looking at something in the trunk of his car. While he was getting ready for bed she went to the garage, opened the trunk, and saw the sack of money. While moving it to a shelf on her side of the closet, a hundred-dollar bill fell out.

"Before shopping this morning, I thought I'd break it into smaller denominations, tens and twenties. It took a while for the teller to return. When she did, Mr. Tracy and a guard were with her. He told the guard to take me to his office." A tear trickled down her cheek. "That's when I learned the bill was part of a money laundering scheme the FBI is investigating." She twisted the handkerchief in her hands, looked at Harold and asked, "What have you done?"

He told her he found the money when he was putting a bundle of newspapers in the trunk to take to work in the morning. He was trying to figure out what to do with it when she saw him. He left out his encounter with Vinny Bling, she was still shaky from dealing with the bank guard.

It was almost noon when Harold pulled in the parking lot of *Rosie's Pizza & Pub*. This wasn't his favorite part of town, he avoided coming here when he could. It was a cloudless day with plenty of sunshine so when he walked in Rosie's it was so dark inside, he could barely see. He smelled of raising dough and tomato sauce.

When trying to make out shapes and objects around him he was greeted by a heavyset man with a tattoo of a battleship on his arm. "I'm Rosie," he said in a husky voice, "what can I get you?"

It took a moment for Harold to adjust, he was under the impression Rosie was a woman. "I'm looking for..." Before he could finish, a voice from a booth in the back of the restaurant called, "Back here Mr. F." Rosie pointed to the man in a three-piece suit holding a glass of iced tea in the air.

When he was seated, Vinny told him to order what he wanted, lunch was on him. Harold thanked him and said he had to get back to work. Vinny said, "A word to the wise Mr. F, never turn down a free lunch." The way he said it convinced Harold the worst thing he could do was refuse the offer.

"What's good?" he asked and it wasn't long before Rosie set a slice of three cheese pizza, a tossed salad, and glass of iced tea in front of him.

"So," Vinny said, "what brings youse to my neck of the woods?"

Harold didn't know where to start. He was sure saying squirrels found the money he'd buried and put it in the trunk of his car would get a laugh and an invitation to leave. Instead, he said, "Bruno was right. When tossed a bundle of newspapers in the dumpster, I saw a grocery bag and looked inside. I did what anyone in a situation like that would do, I took the money home until I could figure out what to do with it. After your visit this morning, I realized I should return it to its rightful owner." He finished with, "It's in the trunk of my car." He stood to go get it, but Vinny stopped him. He snapped his fingers and someone Harold guessed was Bruno, left the booth across from them and went outside.

"He'll need the key to open…" Harold reached in his pocket to get it but stopped when Bruno came in with the grocery bag under his arm. He took it to his booth, looked inside and gave a thumbs up sign in Vinny's direction.

Vinny smiled and said, "Youse has done something for me so what can I do for youse to show my gratitude?"

Harold started to say he couldn't think of anything a gangster being investigated by the FBI for money laundering could do for him, then had a thought. "Do you have connections at city hall?"

Vinny sat back, smiled and said, "Does a fountain pen have ink?" He leaned closer to Harold and asked, "What do youse have in mind?"

When Harold returned to the museum, Dawson was pacing nervously outside his office. The moment he saw Harold he ran to him and said, "Big G changed the timetable for the rally. He says Mayor Blanton is vulnerable and wants to strike while the iron is hot."

Harold groaned, "When is the rally?"

"Saturday afternoon and he expects the platform to be ready," Dawson said.

Harold heard the panic in Dawson's voice, he knew what happened to managers who failed to produce. "What do you have in mind?" he asked.

Dawson looked around to make sure no one was listening before saying, "We have to order material for the platform, cut down the trees, and have it built by Saturday morning."

"You were in the meeting when Big G said he wasn't serious about cutting down the trees," Harold argued. "We could get in trouble doing it without city approval."

"That will take months. The election will be over by then." Dawson moved closer and whispered, "With Big G you have to read between the lines." He pointed to his briefcase and said, "I made a copy of the poster, we can use it to identify which trees have to go."

Harold thought for a moment before saying, "I'll stop by the supply room and get a can of spray paint to mark the trees so we'll know which ones to cut down."

"I guess that's…" Before Dawson could finish, Harold left for the supply room.

They stood in the field, trying to figure out where the platform would be located. Dawson pointed to a place on the poster, Harold said he wasn't sure. Dawson said they should go eight trees deep, Harold felt seven would be enough. When they finally agreed on the size and location of the platform, Harold found an open space on the ground, shook the can of paint, and wrote, "HERE," to let them know how deep in the woods to go. He wrote LEAVE, putting a letter on the trunk of the trees behind where the platform would be located so they wouldn't be included with those they cut down.

As they walked back to the museum, they talked about what needed to be done after building the platform. Should Big G Grocery provide refreshments for those attending the rally? Was that the time to pass out campaign literature? They discussed how many volunteers it would take to get enough signatures to put Big G's name on the ballot, and if they should ask the police to control traffic entering and leaving the parking lot.

Before returning to his office, Harold looked at the message he left and hoped it was enough to let the squirrels know what was going on. While searching for the location of the platform, he saw a nest in one of the trees scheduled to be cut down and hoped there was enough time for them to relocate. If not, at least he tried.

Members of the committee for the protection of neighborhood resources stood in the woods, looking at the marks Harold made.

"I don't get it," one of them said, puzzled by what he saw.

Webster pointed to what was written on the ground and told them the word was here and the marks on the trees spelled leave."

"Here leave?" one of them mumbled, "That makes no sense."

"Why would he say there were leaves here? It's a woods for heaven's sake, there are leaves everywhere" another complained.

"It doesn't say leaves, it says leave," Webster explained than had a thought. What if leave came before here not after? "Seed Man is telling us to leave here."

"The woods?" someone groaned. One more payment and his nest would be paid for.

Webster shook his head. "I don't think so. Just this area where the trees have marks on them."

Dorman looked where he was pointing and nodded. Then, like a light turned on in his mind groaned, "My daughter and her family live here." He pointed to the nest in the top of one of the trees scheduled to be cut down.

Roscoe felt the mood of the committee darken and knew if he didn't say something they would run to the Clearing, tell everyone to pack their bags, they were being thrown out of the woods, and panic would spread. "Guys, we have an evacuation plan. Let's go back to the meeting room and have the safety team walk us through it.

He found Dorman and told him, "We'll get your daughter and her family relocated in time." He wanted to say maybe Seed Man would do something to help but didn't want to build false hopes. Plan for what you know and hope for the best was his motto.

Dawson named it *Operation Woodsman* and was waiting by the dumpster behind the museum when Harold pulled in the parking lot. He got out of his car, walked to where Dawson was standing, and was greeted with, "What took you so long, we should have started an hour ago."

Harold apologized, said he didn't own a chain saw and had to borrow his neighbor's. Dawson gave him a bundle of rope and told him to get the can of gasoline from the trunk of his car, he'd take the saws to the woods.

Harold said he'd meet him there and left for his car. Dawson told him to make it snappy, they didn't have all night as he picked up the saws and started across the field. When he reached the trees, the generator Ryan brought to take a picture of the symbol intended for the find the nut tournament, started and a bank of lights came on, temporarily blinding him.

When his sight returned, he heard sirens in the distance and figured the police were chasing someone who'd run a red light or was speeding. He was looking for the trees Harold marked when a patrol car pulled in the parking lot. He wasn't concerned, someone probably reported an unauthorized vehicle was parked there.

The first shiver of panic came when the patrol car didn't stop in the parking lot but continued across the field, moving in his direction. If it weren't for the lights, he could hide in the woods until they were gone. The way it was, he stuck out like a butternut squash in the sweet potato section. He tossed the saws in the woods and was removing incriminating evidence from his backpack when a police officer, speaking through a bullhorn, told him to, "Get on your knees, and put your hands in the air."

He did and soon was surrounded by policemen with their weapons drawn. The chief of police stepped forward and asked if he knew he was about to destroy the habitat of an endangered species. He held up a cease-and-desist order signed by Judge Bascom that afternoon.

Dawson tried to come up with an explanation for why he was in the field at midnight with a chain saw. When he couldn't he said, "Harold Finebender will vouch for me. We were just…" His confidence took another blow when he saw Harold pull out of the parking lot and onto the street in front of the museum.

Big G watched the scene play out from the window in his office on the second floor. Especially the part where Harold left when the police arrived. He wondered what there was about the woods that blocked everything he tried to do there? The turkey hunt. The shopping promotion. And now, the platform for the political rally.

All great ideas that failed. He was sure Harold had something to do with it but didn't think he was smart enough to pull it off on his own, he had help.

When the last police car left the field, he decided if Dawson couldn't get the job done, he would. He walked out the backdoor and got as far as the dumpster when someone asked, "You Big G?' He squinted because the light on back of the building was still on, all he could make out was the outline of a man leaning against the hood of a late model car.

"What's it to you?' he growled. He had work to do and didn't have time to talk to a stranger.

"That's our guy," the stranger said, and snapped his fingers. A member of Vinny's gang grabbed Big G from behind and tied his hands with rope he found where Harold's car was parked. With no chance for Big G to escape, Bruno picked him up, threw him over his shoulder, and carried him to his car.

Ferrel stopped when he reached the edge of the parking lot and breathed in the familiar air. He smiled when he saw the floodlights, still on from the midnight raid by the police, lighting his way to the woods. He wasn't sure how they pulled it off, no one knew he was coming. The concert season was over, and he was returning home for some much-needed rest and relaxation. The problem facing him now was how to react when community members came out to greet him. Should he be surprised? Act like he was expecting them?

He was halfway across the field when the generator ran out of gasoline, sputtered, and stopped. The lights flickered, then turned off. With the lights off and no one to greet him, he was sure his welcome home party was planned by the committee, they couldn't even get this right.

The next morning Harold slowed when he entered the parking lot, puzzled when he saw Big G department managers huddled at the entrance of the museum. Yellow police tape stretched across the door and to make sure people took it seriously, a policeman stood on the front steps with his arms across his chest, daring anyone to get by him.

When he reached the front of the building, he approached the managers and asked, "What's going on?"

"Dawson's in jail." "Big G is missing." "Investigators are going through the file cabinet in his office." They said at the same time.

Harold decided the best thing for him to do was go home and return when employees were allowed back in the building. He hadn't slept well after getting home last night and could use a nap. As he pulled out of his parking place, he realized in his hurry to leave he hadn't provided a way for the squirrels to get in the trunk of his car. He didn't have any newspapers to take to the dumpster anyway and made a mental note to get a bundle ready when he got home.

As he approached his house, he saw Bruno sitting in a car across from his driveway and wondered what he was doing there. He waved and Bruno returned the greeting by touching the brim of his hat.

He pulled in the garage, got out, gathered newspapers in a bundle, and tied them with twine. He carried them to his car, opened the trunk, and found Big G curled up inside. He was bound and gagged and had a bruise on his forehead from bumping into something.

He removed the ropes and helped him up. Sitting in the trunk, with his hair messed up and without a cigar in his mouth, he looked like a normal guy. Maybe it was because the managers weren't around. Maybe it was because he looked defeated. More than likely it was because he was sitting in the Harold's garage and not at the bottom of a landfill on the outskirts of town.

Harold heard a car motor start and looked in time to see Bruno ease away from the curb and start down the street.

Vinny was in his usual booth at Rosie's, having lunch with a friend when his phone played the theme from *The Godfather*, letting him know he had a message. He glanced at the screen, saw it was from Bruno and read, "Package opened."

He smiled, put the phone in his pocket and told Rosie, "Iced tea for everyone. I'm buying."

TAKE ME OUT OF THE BALL GAME

Harold was almost to his car when the back door of the museum opened and Officer Gardner hollered, "Big G called a meeting. He wants everyone in his office in five minutes."

Harold stood with a hand on the car door. It had been a busy day. Since the incident with the ambassador, everyone wanted to see the pen and hear its incredible story. And he was trying to wrap things up before going on vacation. It was more of a busman's holiday; he and Thelma were going to the Fountain Pen Convention in Parker, Pennsylvania.

He was about to ask him to tell Big G he was too late, when he got to the parking lot he was gone when Dawson pushed passed Officer Gardner and said, "Thank goodness I caught you, Big G is waiting."

Things never went well for Harold at a Big G meeting. Although he wasn't part of what Big G called his A Team, he ended up involved with whatever was planned.

He was the last to enter the crowded office and found Big G and the managers wearing orange baseball caps with a blue *BGG* on the front. Dawson handed him one and pointed to his head, telling him with the gesture to put it on.

Big G motioned for Dawson to close the door, and while walking to the window said, "We sell hot dogs and soda pop." He waited a moment, then spun around and asked, "What ain't we got?"

The department managers were stumped. Was he talking about a special promotion? A sale on the items he mentioned? A new line of products for the grocery store?

"Buy me some peanuts and cracker jacks," Big G sang, slightly off key.

One of the managers started to leave to get the items he mentioned but stopped when Big G said, "Thoughts Finebender?"

"From the items you mentioned and the caps we're wearing, I'll take a wild guess and say it has something to do with baseball."

"And?" Big G asked, disappointed Harold figured it out before the managers had.

Harold shrugged, he had no idea where he was going with this and wondered why every meeting started with Big G expecting the managers to guess why they were there.

"You're taking us to a game?" "You're forming a team? "You're having Big G Day at..." The manager with the last suggestion stopped when Big G removed the stub of a cigar from his mouth, pointed the soggy end it at him, and motioned for him to continue.

He was stuck. He hadn't played baseball as a kid and was on the debate team in high school. The college he attended didn't have an athletic program because, as it stated in the student handbook, "You are here to learn not waste time on frivolous pursuits that have no practical application after you graduate."

Big G returned to the window. "You get out of your car, walk across the parking lot, look up and see," he reached down and lifted a poster from behind his desk. It was a drawing of a stadium and, above the entrance, was an electronic sign welcoming fans to the *Big G SportsPlex*.

He expected an enthusiastic response but got blank looks and open mouths. "It's called synergy," he explained like he was talking to a group of grade school students, "bringing products we sell to an audience who buys them."

The managers got that part, but it seemed like a lot of work just to sell a few hot dogs.

"Where will the ballpark be located?" Harold asked, breaking the uncomfortable silence in the room.

"SportsPlex," Big G corrected him. "It's called a SportsPlex because other sports will be played there like rugby and flag football. But to answer your question, it will be located where I spent many pleasant hours as a youth. It's where I learned winning requires hard work, total commitment, and sliding into third base with your spikes in the air." He knew he'd lost them, so he said in frustration,

"I bought Dogood Field and next spring the gates of the *Big G SportsPlex* will open to start a fabulous new season."

One of the managers raised a hand and said, "Dogood Field is a dump sir. I drive by it on the way to work. Half the bleachers are missing, and the scoreboard is about to fall down. It doesn't look anything like that." He pointed to the drawing Big G was holding.

The other managers asked, "Aren't there fields in better condition for sale?" "Did you look into the financial side of the operation?" "Did you think it through or were you operating on emotion and old memories?" Two things Big G warned them against when making important decisions.

Big G ignored their comments and said proudly, "When construction is finished, other fields in the city won't be in our league."

"Dogood Field," Harold repeated quietly and wondered what there was about the name that stuck in his mind? He remembered going there when he was working at *Finebruners Fine Writing Instruments*. A client invited him to watch his daughter play a softball game there. The field had no lights, so when the game went into extra innings and it was too dark for the batter to see the ball leave the pitcher's hand, the umpire declared it a draw, there was no winner.

He shook his head, that wasn't it. There was something else... involving... squirrels. Two lived there and survived by eating food spectators threw in the trash cans. The other thing he remembered was, they were so used to being around humans they allowed children to pick them up and stroke their fur.

He straightened when the thought hit him. What will happen to the squirrels when the ballfield is replaced with a new one?

"Do you have something to say?" Big G asked when he saw Harold staring at the drawing and rubbing his chin, deep in thought.

Harold shrugged and said, "Nothing others haven't mentioned." The last thing he wanted was for Big G to find out what he was thinking.

As the managers were leaving the meeting, Big G grunted, "Dawson. A word." He closed the door and growled, "I don't trust

Finebender any farther than I can throw him. I want you to stick to him like peanut butter on a saltine. Got it?"

Dawson nodded and hurried out of the room, hoping to catch Harold before he reached the parking lot.

Tobias Dogood was a tireless worker, balancing two jobs with an occasional third, pumping gas at a filling station on weekends. As busy as he was, he found time to promote little league baseball. He hadn't played when he was a kid, he was busy with schoolwork and doing odd jobs in the neighborhood to support his ailing parents. As a result, he felt he'd missed something important. He read everything he could about the sport and been a mentor and friend to hundreds of kids in the neighborhood. When his health declined and he couldn't coach anymore, he became a spectator, sitting in the stands in August, wrapped in a blanket to ward off the chill.

When his will was read, no one was surprised to learn he gave the field he owned to the Centerline Little League. In addition to the field, there was money for bleachers, a fence behind home plate, and a scoreboard. Unfortunately, there wasn't enough for lights, so tournaments and championship games were played somewhere else.

At the dedication, the president of the little league announced it would be named *Dogood Field* in honor of the benefactor. A place on the bleachers was painted gold in appreciation for his gift to the youth of Centerline. No matter how crowded the stands, no one sat in the place honoring Tobias Dogood.

After the ballfield was built, parents of the kids in the league took turns dragging the infield before games, taking tickets, and selling refreshments.

Along with being an avid baseball fan, Tobias loved wildlife and, on his few days off, he could be found on the plot of land he owned filling bird feeders and trimming low hanging branches to make it easier for larger animals to get around. When time permitted, he'd sit with his back against the trunk of a tree and encourage birds to pick seeds from his hand. The animals who called the field home assumed all humans were as kind and friendly as him. When the feeders were taken down and the trees removed to make way for the ball field, the birds decided there was no reason to hang around and moved to more promising territory.

Squirrels lived on the land before Tobias bought it, so they stayed to see what it would be like when the construction was over. One by one they wandered away, unwilling to wait when they realized tradition was the only thing keeping them from leaving. Trucks driven by construction workers were noisy and made it dangerous for them to go from one part of the field to the other.

Two remained, finding enough to eat from the workers discarded lunches to maintain their simple lifestyle. When the field was ready for play, they feasted on popcorn and hot dog buns dropped from the bleachers. With the trees gone they looked for a place to live and found it in a long tube surrounded by a tarpaulin the humans pulled across the field when it rained.

Living in the tube was inconvenient, but baseball was played during the summer, the rest of the year the tarp remained near the home team dugout. Enough tee shirts and towels were left by players to stuff in the ends of the tube during cold weather, leaving the inside as warm and comfortable as the nest they lived in before the field was built.

So, Ernest and Emily, the names of the squirrels who stayed when others left, set up house in their unusual nest, dividing it into living and sleeping areas and securing furniture so it wouldn't break the few times a year the tarp was used.

During the baseball season, Ernest would stand beside the tarp with a paw over his heart like the humans did when the national anthem was played at the start of a game. When twins were born, he named them Free and Brave, names taken from the anthem he listened to.

Growing up the boys knew nothing about the lives of squirrels their age. They'd never climbed a tree or foraged for acorns. They wouldn't know how to build a nest if their lives depended on it, they assumed all squirrels lived in tubes because it was all they knew.

When Ernest attended seed school, he took an HSL (Human as a Second Language) class and during the winter, when it was too cold to play outside, he shared what he remembered with his sons.

While Ernest and Emily were satisfied puttering around inside the tube, the boys weren't.

During the summer, the field was used almost every day so when they weren't busy collecting food humans dropped and storing it in an opening in the back of the scoreboard, they sat beside the tarp and watched the young humans' play.

One day, after the anthem was sung and before the umpire shouted, "Play ball," Free left his place by the tarp, sprinted across the field, and slid into second base like he'd seen the young humans do. He stood, brushed the dirt off his fur, and jogged off the field to the cheers of delighted spectators.

It was exhilarating. He'd never felt anything like it. When he crossed the foul line, he jumped into the arms of his less adventurous brother. For the rest of the game, they sat with their backs against the tarp, munching peanuts from a bag a spectator threw in their direction.

It wasn't long before it became part of the pre-game routine at Dogood Field. After singing the anthem, the spectators remained standing and chanted, "Squirrel, squirrel," until Free left his place by the tarp, ran across the field, and slid into second base. After dusting himself off, he raised his arms in the air, a gesture that brought more cheers and applause.

After each performance, food was tossed their way and what they didn't eat, they stored in the hiding place in the back of the scoreboard.

Over time the number of games played at Dogood Field decreased, teams preferred to play at the more up-to-date field built by Centerline Parks and Recreation. It had all the amenities players wanted; a fence around the outfield, enclosed dugouts so they didn't have to sit in the sun for nine innings and lights for games in August when it was too hot to play during the day.

The day after Big G announced constructing the SportsPlex, Harold was about to leave for the day when Dawson asked if he'd give him a ride home. "My car is in the shop," he explained. Harold said he'd be happy to. As they were leaving the parking lot, Harold saw Dawson's car parked behind two others. Okay, he thought as traffic cleared and he pulled on the street, I see what's going on. "How do I get to your place?" he asked.

"I don't want to be an inconvenience, so I asked a friend to pick me up at your house," Dawson said and increased the volume on the radio, making further conversation impossible.

As he drove home, Harold realized any attempt to do something for the squirrels at Dogood Field would not go unnoticed. With Dawson sharing his office, he'd listen to every phone conversation and report what he heard to Big G.

When he reached his house, Harold looked around and said, "I don't see your friend?"

Dawson held up his phone and said, "He sent a text saying he's running late. I'll wait in front of your house if it's okay." He got out and Harold continued down the driveway.

After closing the garage door, he sat in the car thinking if he was going to save the squirrels, he needed help. Contacting Lloyd Brewster was out of the question, Big G had probably instructed the store manager to let him know the moment he showed up.

He needed a go between, someone they wouldn't suspect. He blinked in surprise when Thelma's name popped in his mind.

During the evening meal he looked for a way to direct the conversation to the problem at Dogood Field as she talked about something she heard at the beauty parlor or the telephone call she received from Sylvia, Myron Boggs wife.

By dessert he was getting desperate, if he didn't say something soon, she would be in front of the television, watching her favorite show. This was the seventh season, and she hadn't missed an episode. No conversation was allowed except during commercials. Then it was limited to, "Be a dear and make popcorn," or, "A bowl of ice cream would taste good."

It was now or never so he folded his napkin, put it by his plate and said, "I need help."

"What's that dear?" she asked as she leafed through a catalog that came in the mail.

He reached over, closed the catalog and repeated, "I need help."

His comment took her by surprise. In thirty years of marriage, he'd only asked for her help once. He was on a ladder and said, "Hand me the Phillips head screwdriver?"

She took his hand in hers, looked him in the eye and said, "You have my undivided attention."

Get on with it he told himself, get the hard part over with. If she refuses, you'll have time to think of someone else. "It involves squirrels. Two actually."

She sat back like she'd been sprayed with a garden hose. She recovered and said sympathetically, "They're gone dear. You've seen the sign at the entrance declaring Sunny Hill Estates is squirrel free."

He started with, "Big G bought a baseball field," and didn't stop until he said someone had to contact Lloyd Brewster and tell him what was going on.

"Who?" she asked. She glanced at the clock and realized she'd missed the first half of *Dotty Pellligrue, MD*.

Harold told her how he met Lloyd and what a bright young man he was. All she had to do was explain the situation with the squirrels to him, he'd take it from there.

"Where do I find him?" she asked with little enthusiasm.

Harold tore a page from the catalog, wrote Lloyd's name on it, and drew a map showing the location of the store where he worked. Before giving her the paper, he added the address of *Rosie's Pizza and Pub*. Along with the information he wrote, "Ask for Vinny Bling. He's in the second booth on the right."

As she read the note, she pointed at what he'd written about Vinny and asked, "What's that?"

"It's a backup. A worst-case scenario in case Lloyd isn't available."

She gasped when she saw the address. "Isn't that in..."

Harold told her, "If you go at noon, you'll have nothing to worry about. Tell Rosie you have a message for Vinny."

"What if one of my..."

He was going to tell her the chance of one of her friends being in that part of town was slim but didn't when he realized she wasn't listening. The last thing he heard before getting up to clear dishes from the table was her saying, "A message for Vinny?"

The next morning when Harold pulled out of the garage and started up the driveway, he saw Dawson sitting on the steps in front of his house. He waved as he walked unsteadily to the car, got in, yawned, and said, "My friend dropped me off."

Harold started to ask if it wouldn't have been easier for his friend to take him to work when he noticed he hadn't shaved and the coffee stain on the cuff of his shirt yesterday, was still there. Apparently, Dawson slept on the steps in front of his house in case he tried to go out in the middle of the night. Harold wondered if there was anything he wouldn't do for Big G.

He parked in his reserved place and waited until Dawson reached the backdoor of the museum before hollering, "I forgot something, I'll be right back." He left his parking place and started toward the street. He glanced at the rearview mirror and saw Dawson running after him. When he realized he couldn't catch him on foot he hesitated, considered his options, then ran to his car,

Harold turned before reaching the street, parked behind a van, slid down in the seat and waited.

Dawson stopped when he reached the street wondering which way Harold went, then pulled into the morning traffic, hoping to catch him before he'd gone far.

Harold smiled as he pulled in his parking place, got out, and strolled contentedly to the rear entrance.

Big G was in the Grand Hall talking to one of the managers When he saw Harold come in alone, he growled, "Where's Dawson?"

Harold shrugged, said, "I didn't know it was my day to watch him," punched in the code, entered the security room, and closed the door.

Free woke to a sound different than the usual traffic noise from the street in front of Dogood Field. He went to the edge of the tube, looked out, and saw a vehicle with a scoop on the front moving across the infield toward the tarp. He woke Brave and was grabbing all the family momentous he could carry when the tube shook.

They reached the end of the tube as it was being lifted in the air, leaped to the ground, and watched in despair as the machine rolled across the field and dropped the only home they'd known in a dumpster.

"Get the food," Free shouted to his brother. They'd crossed the first base foul line when the scoreboard buckled and fell in what used to be center field.

Shortly after Harold left for work, Thelma drove to the Big G grocery store in Jackson Hollow. This was new territory for her, she shopped at *The Groceria*, a natural food store nearer her house. She pulled in the parking lot, took the first available space, put on the blond wig she'd worn to a costume party years ago and added a hat with a brim she pulled down to cover part of her face. To complete the disguise, she slipped on a pair of sunglasses and practiced what she was going to say in a voice lower than normal. "I'm looking for Lloyd Brewster, I was told he works here."

She got out of the car, walked to the entrance, stopped the first worker she came to and repeated what she practiced in the car. She got as far as, "Lloyd Brewster," when the worker said, "He doesn't work here anymore."

She took off the sunglasses and said in surprise, "Doesn't work here?"

The worker shook her head.

"When..."

The worker called to the woman at the cash register, "How long has Lloyd been gone?"

The woman said, "A week. Maybe two," then turned to the customer she was helping and asked, "Did you find everything okay?"

"But I..." Thelma stammered as the worker walked away.

"This can't be happening," she mumbled as she walked to her car. With the grocery store out of the picture she was left with the worst-case scenario, she would talk to Vinny Bling.

She drove by *Rosie's Pizza and Pub* twice before convincing herself to go through with it. She was sure someone she knew would see her entering an establishment she would normally avoid like the plague. She checked her appearance in the rearview mirror. The blond wig was in place, the brim of her hat pulled down and the heavily tinted sunglasses shielded her eyes.

She hesitated as she got out of the car when she saw two rough looking men standing near the entrance, smoking cigarettes. She pressed on. She promised Harold she'd do it so she would, but he'd get an earful when he got home. She was almost to the door when one of the men moved away from the other, said, "Allow me," and opened it.

It was dark inside under normal conditions, but the sunglasses made it impossible for her to see. She tripped over the first step and would have fallen if she hadn't been caught by a man cleaning tables. "Hey. Hey. Easy does it," he said and held her arm until she regained her balance. When he was sure she was okay he said, "I'm Rosie, what can I get for you?"

She removed the sunglasses and looked around. Harold told her Vinny would be in the second booth on the right, but it was empty. "Where's Vinny?" she asked in a husky voice, hoping to keep her identity secret.

"He doesn't come in on Thursday," Rosie said as he stepped behind the counter. She started to say someone told her he ate lunch here every day. Before she could, Rosie pointed to a man in another booth and told her, "His righthand man Bruno is over there."

"I don't think..." she stammered, turned to leave and was almost to the door, when a large man in a pin stripped suite stepped in front of her and said, "I'm Bruno," as he took her arm and led her to his booth.

Once seated, he leaned toward her, opened his hands, and asked, "So, why do you want to see Vinny?"

"I'm Isabelle Brewster and am, ah, looking for my son Lloyd. I was told Vinny has ways of finding people."

Bruno studied her for a moment, unfolded a piece of paper the man who opened the door for her gave him when she was talking to Rosie. He shook his head, disappointed she hadn't been honest with him. "It says here you're Thelma Finebender, live in Sunny Hill Estates and have no kids. One of my boys ran a trace on your license plate." He reached over, removed the hat and wig, tossed them on the seat beside her and asked, "What do you say we start over? I'm Bruno. Why the getup?"

Thelma pushed the wrapper of a straw around the table with her finger. How dare he run the numbers on her license plate without her permission. How dare he remove her hat and wig without asking.

Bruno broke the silence with, "I am familiar with your husband, we worked together on a, ah, recent project,"

With her cover blown, there was no reason to pretend anymore. "Harold is looking for a young man named Lloyd Brewster," she said in her regular voice.

"Why does he want to find him?" Bruno asked.

She'd hoped to avoid this part. Before the developer cut down trees to build more homes in her subdivision, she'd used every means available to get rid of the squirrels in their yard. The only blemish on her otherwise perfect driving record came when she was stopped for reckless driving because she thought there were squirrels in the trunk of her car.

"It involves… squirrels. Two actually." After saying it the rest of the story rolled out effortlessly. At the mention of Big G's name Bruno raised an eyebrow, other than that, he listened but showed no emotion.

"That's it," she said and lifted her hands, letting him know she was finished. "Big G is keeping an eye on Harold. He thought if Lloyd found out what was going on he'd help."

Bruno nodded slowly, thinking about what she said. He waved to Rosie and said, "Two lunch specials with," he looked at Thelma and asked, "how do you like your iced tea? Sweetened or plain?"

They were almost finished eating when a large man wearing a sport coat over a turtleneck sweater, walked to their table and whispered something in Bruno's ear. Bruno nodded, turned to Thelma, and said, "While we have enjoyed a pleasant meal, my boys have made inquiries and located Lloyd."

"How did they... I mean how could..."

"I am not at liberty to divulge our source of information but the person in question lives above the Big G grocery store in Jackson Hollow." Bruno sat back and flashed a satisfied smile.

"That's not possible," Thelma protested. "I went there, and a worker said he was gone, hadn't been seen in weeks."

Bruno, unfazed by her response said, "You asked for Lloyd Brewster?"

Thelma nodded.

"That was your first mistake. To reach Lloyd, go to the pharmacy and say you're there to pick up a prescription for Mr. Finebender."

"Harold didn't say I was to..."

Bruno waved his large hands and said, "He doesn't know. It's a recent development." He escorted her to the door, pointed to the two men outside and said, "Rocky and Duke will walk you to your car in case you were followed."

"In case I was..." Thelma looked around nervously as she was escorted to her car.

She reluctantly returned to Big G Grocery store, this time without a disguise. She waited while the pharmacist explained to a customer what to expect from the medicine she'd purchased. "Should I eat this with food?" she asked. The pharmacist pointed to the sticker on the bottle that said, *Do Not Take On An Empty Stomach.*

When she left, Thelma took her place and the pharmacist asked, "How can I help you?" She said she was there to pick up a prescription for Mr. Finebender. He looked at her, trying to decide if she was on the up and up.

"I'm his wife. I have identification if..." He stopped her with, "That won't be necessary," and handed her a small white sack. Stapled to it was a hastily written note that told her to go to the back of the store, knock twice on a door marked *Employees Only* and say, "Cleanup on aisle three."

When she turned to go the pharmacist stopped her with, "Sorry about the cloak and dagger stuff but Lloyd's a special kid. We feel he was treated unfairly when Big G fired him. We're doing everything we can to make sure he doesn't kick him out of the apartment." He pointed to a wall at the back of the store.

She thanked him and walked down aisles, looking at products, trying to be as inconspicuous as possible. The last thing she wanted was for someone she knew to see her and say, "I didn't know you shopped here?"

When she reached the door, she knocked twice and said, "Cleanup on aisle three." When she didn't get an answer, she started to walk away thinking Lloyd wasn't home. The door opened a crack and a worried looking young man said, "Yes?"

He didn't recognize her and was about to close the door when she said, "I'm Mrs. Finebender, Harold's wife. He's being followed and sent me to..." Before she finished, he motioned for to come in. As soon as she was inside, he closed the door and slid the dead bolt in place.

She followed him up a flight of steps and down a narrow hallway to his apartment. Once inside, he removed an electronic parts catalog from a chair, sat on the bed across from her and asked, "Why are you here?"

Why indeed she wondered. She'd done some crazy things in her life but nothing like this. Meeting with gangsters in a shady part of town and using a secret code to reach a boy she'd never met to help a creature that had caused her more grief and expense than anyone could imagine.

When she didn't answer he asked, "Are you okay?"

She nodded she was and took a breath before saying, "There's a ballpark not far from here."

"Dogood Field. I played on a little league team there one summer." He looked at the floor, shrugged his shoulders, and said solemnly, "Coach Berm didn't ask me back the next year."

"There are, if I understand the situation correctly, two squirrels who…"

"They were great. After the national anthem one would run across the field and slide into second base." He shook his head and said quietly, "I forgot about them."

"Big G bought the field and is tearing it down to build a SportsPlex. Harold was afraid…"

Lloyd was out of his chair and heading for the door. "Tell Mr. Finebender I'll… I mean, tell him I'm on it." Then he was gone, leaving Thelma alone in a cluttered apartment, wondering how to leave without being seen by someone she knew.

Free and Brave clung to each other not sure what to do. The only home they'd known was gone, and the place where they stored their food was a mass of twisted steel in the outfield. They stood with their backs against what was left of the fence behind where home plate had been. Free tapped Brave on the shoulder and pointed to three construction workers walking toward them. They'd spread out, approaching from three sides to cut off escape routes.

As they moved closer to the trembling squirrels, they picked rocks and clods of dirt from what had once been the infield. The one in the middle told the other two, "Take your time boys, the boss left for a meeting and won't be back until after lunch."

Free couldn't understand what he said but didn't have to, it was obvious he and his brother were in trouble.

The workers reached the pitcher's mound when a kid on a bicycle sailed by them, skidded to a stop, scooped up the frightened squirrels, and put them in a basket attached to the handlebars.

"Wrong move kid. You just gave us another target." The one who appeared to be the leader told the others. "I'll take the kid; you get the squirrels."

"Or not," someone behind him said. When he turned around, he saw three of the meanest looking men he'd ever seen walking toward him.

"No. We, ah, saw the squirrels and were helping the kid..." The leader did his best to come up with an excuse for what they were doing but wasn't up to the task.

"Did you get the package?" Bruno asked Lloyd, not intimidated by the construction workers, for him it was another day at the office.

"The package?" Lloyd asked, realized he was talking about the squirrels and said, "Yes. Got it."

"I suggest you take off, it could get a little messy here. Right boys?" Bruno asked. The two with him grunted they agreed.

"You got it wrong pal. We were just horsing around. We weren't going to..." The leader of the workers stammered as he looked for a way to escape.

Lloyd asked Bruno how he knew he was here. "I got a call from Thelma. She said she thought you could use our help."

"Thelma?" Lloyd repeated, the name meant nothing to him.

"Mrs. Finebender," Bruno said then told him, "Scram. It's time for us to go to work."

Lloyd thanked him for showing up when he did and rode away as fast as his one speed bicycle would go. He didn't look back to check on the fate of the construction workers, he'd accomplished what he came for, the squirrels were safe.

As he pedaled back to the grocery store and the safety of his apartment, he didn't notice the car half a block behind him. It followed him to the store and when she was sure he was safely inside, Thelma drove home, anxious to tell Harold all that had gone on.

The next day she returned to Lloyd's apartment to talk about what to do with the squirrels, he couldn't keep them here. After exploring several possibilities, they decided the *Children's Zoo of Centerline* was the perfect place for them.

A few days after taking them there, Thelma received a call from the director of the zoo who said there was a problem. The purpose of the petting zoo was to allow children to see the animals up close but so far, the squirrels have refused to leave the nest the zoo built for them.

She called Lloyd and told Lloyd about the director's call.

After making sure the coast was clear, Lloyd ran across the loading dock and jumped in the backseat of her car. When they got to the zoo, he saw the problem. The squirrels were in a nest not a tube. The director said she'd take care of it if he could get them to come out and mingle with the children. If they didn't, they'd have to take them someplace else.

Lloyd thought for a moment then took out his phone. He found the national anthem in the directory, turned the volume to high, and hit play. The song could be heard around the park and the children hurried over to see what was going on. When the music stopped Free hopped out of the nest, ran across the open space, and slid into a paper plate Lloyd put there. He stood, dusted off his fur, and lifted his paws in the air.

The children cheered.

Free slowly turned, absorbing their applause, then jogged back to Brave who was holding a sack of roasted peanuts a worker put there to coax them out of the nest.

They hugged and realized they were home; they were going to be okay.

Big G sat across from the recently completed *Big G SportsPlex* trying to figure out what was wrong. The stadium was finished on time and under budget. Inside was everything a fan or player could want from heated seats in the dugout for chilly spring mornings, to a food court that put the one at the *Great Mall of Centerline* to shame.

The problem was no team had signed up to play there, the league commissioner hadn't returned his calls and, from the day it opened, protesters showed up, demanding the name be changed to the *Dogood SportsPlex* and that he bring the squirrels back.

The last part about squirrels caused him to wonder if, in spite Dawson watching him day and night for the last three weeks, Harold was involved. But how could he be? Dawson had been with him the whole time. His last thought before tapping on the window and telling the driver to move on was maybe he'd been watching the wrong person. He wrote in his notebook to have a talk with Dawson the moment he got back to his office.

IF OPPORTUNITY KNOCKS, DON'T OPEN THE DOOR

"Mister Chairman, we meet at last," the visitor said as he crossed the room with a paw extended.

Roscoe entered the meeting room thinking of all he had to do before the morning committee meeting. It took a moment for him to shift from his agenda to a stranger walking toward him.

The one who greeted him followed with, "I'm J. Jay with *Nest 2 Nest Communications.*" He pointed to the tall, thin person standing by the window, "That is my associate, E.A. Poe."

E.A. touched his forehead with a paw.

While Roscoe waited for more information like, what they were doing in the meeting room without being invited, he studied the stranger. He was short, heavyset, wore a plaid vest, and had arranged the fur on his head to cover a bald spot. The visitor broke the silence with, "My friends call me JJ."

"The sound the same, don't they?" Roscoe said as he moved to his desk and wrote the committee needed to revisit the open-door policy on a notepad. If it had been closed these two would be outside, waiting in the Clearing.

"I'm sorry?" The stranger said, confused by the comment.

"Your name and what your friends call you?" Roscoe noticed his planner was open and turned, facing where JJ was standing when he entered the room.

JJ thought for a moment then burst into laughter. "Good one Mr. Chairman. I'll have to bring my A game if I'm going to keep up with you." He removed a card from a pocket of his vest with the *Nest 2 Nest* logo on the front; a circle of nests connected by a wire and handed it to Roscoe. Beneath the company name was their mission statement, *Bringing neighborhoods together one community at a time.*

"I'm sorry gentlemen but I have a meeting..." Roscoe stopped when JJ said, "I know." It wasn't followed by, "Oops, you caught me looking at your planner, so I know exactly what's on your schedule today," just, "I know."

"If you will talk to my secretary..."

"She won't be coming in, I gave her the morning off," JJ said as if sending someone who doesn't work for you home was the most natural thing in the world.

"You gave her..." Roscoe stammered.

"The morning off. Yes." JJ said and gestured for E.A. Poe to stand in front of the door to prevent anyone from entering during his presentation.

"Why would you..."

JJ strolled confidently to the small window above the wooden bench, looked out, and watched the activity in the Clearing before saying, "There are moments in the life of a community when a single decision determines its future." He turned to face Roscoe and said solemnly, "This is that moment Mr. Chairman. You can be the catalyst for change, the visionary who, with the stroke of a pen will put your community on the path to a glorious future or fall behind your neighbors who have embraced the technology we offer."

He held out a paw. E.A. Poe rushed over and put a device the size of a deck of cards in it. "On the floor, next to your desk, is what we call the Central Control Unit." He waited for Roscoe to look where he was pointing before continuing. "The CCU, working in tandem with the receiver I'm holding," he paused, allowing the significance of his message to build, "will move your community from the shallows of mediocrity into the mainstream of commerce."

Roscoe heard someone bump against the door and give a surprised yelp when it didn't open. The sound was followed by a muffled, "Roscoe? Are you in there?"

JJ didn't seem to notice as he lifted the receiver, pressed a button and said, "Chairman Ben, are you there sir?"

His question was followed by a burst of static. Roscoe heard Ben mutter, "I hear him, which button do I press to answer?" A voice

Roscoe didn't recognize said, "The green one." There was more muttering then Ben said, "Roscoe? Can you hear me?"

JJ offered Roscoe the receiver, but he waved him off. JJ shrugged and said, "Chairman Ben, this is JJ in the Community of Abner. How's the weather where you are?" It was meant as a conversation starter, but Ben thought he was genuinely interested, although the two communities are less than a hundred yards apart.

"Well, let's see. It's ..." Roscoe heard a door open, and Ben say, "warm. Humid. There's a light breeze from the..."

"Sorry to interrupt Mr. Chairman but would you read from the script my associate gave you this morning?" JJ asked impatiently. Roscoe heard muffled voices and the sound of papers turning then, "Is it the one that says *A Test of the Nest 2 Nest Communication System*, or *The Owner's Manual for Ordering Parts?*"

"The first," JJ said and turned the receiver so Roscoe could hear.

"I don't know where..." Ben stammered. Someone said, "Start here sir."

"Oh right. Okay." He cleared his throat and began. "I'd like to meet with you tomorrow morning. Will you check your schedule to see if you're available?"

Out of habit, Roscoe glanced at his planner then remembered this was a demonstration.

JJ answered, "I'm meeting with Principal Charles in the morning, how does your afternoon look?"

"The afternoon is good. I'll see you then." There was more static, and Roscoe heard Ben ask, "How do I turn it off. I can't..." Then it was quiet.

JJ pushed the blue button on the receiver and stood quietly, giving Roscoe time to think about what he heard. "By my count Mr. Chairman, I achieved in seconds what would have taken Bem's secretary three trips between the two communities to accomplish. The first with the request for a meeting. A second with the suggested change. And a final trip to confirm the time of the appointment." He walked to Roscoe's desk, placed the receiver next to the central control unit and said, "I'm sure someone in your position can see the benefit of instant communication between communities. The time saved in this simple demonstration will be measured in hours, not minutes when the unit is installed." He waited a moment before saying, "Would you like to contact the Highly Exalted Chairman? Have a three-way conversation between him, Ben, and you?"

Ferrel slept late after his trip home and was on his way to *Out On A Limb* for a piece of nut cake and a cup of walnut tea when he saw members of the committee standing on the platform outside the meeting room. He walked over, touched paws with each of them and asked, "What's going on?"

Lothar pointed to the door and said, "It's closed. We're locked out."

Roscoe heard noise on the platform as committee members grew restless and demanded to know what was going on.

"I need to," before Roscoe could say, "let them in," JJ said, "Allow me," and motioned for E.A. Poe to open the door.

Having nothing better to do, Ferrel followed the committee inside, curious about the closed door and the strangers inside.

The list of items Roscoe had highlighted in his planner that needed immediate attention was abandoned as JJ introduced himself to the committee and gave each of them a complimentary dessert coupon for *Out On A Limb*. He went into his sales pitch, walking around the room, explaining the advantage of signing up for the *Nest 2 Nest* Community Benefit Package. Warnings could be sent if danger was headed their way. An announcement from the COC informing them of a policy change would arrive instantly rather than delivered the next day. "And" JJ said as he punched a button on the receiver, "how about a little background music to help meetings run smoothly?"

Classical music came from the receiver JJ placed in the middle of the conference table. He stepped back, encouraged committee members to examine the device and contemplate the unlimited possibilities a membership with *Nest 2 Nest* offered.

No one said anything. Even Ferrel, usually the first to offer an opinion, was silent, overwhelmed by what he heard. If it was possible to read their thoughts, Roscoe would have seen a single question; how soon can we get our paws on one of those?

Roscoe broke the silence with, "Thank you JJ. You've given us a lot to think about." They were almost to the door when Ferrel stepped in front of them and said, "Hold on. You're not leaving until you tells us what a unit like those costs."

"The price for leasing the equipment is fifteen seeds," JJ said matter-of-factly and heard a murmur from committee members, surprised at the cost. "In addition, there is a monthly maintenance fee of five seeds." He raised a paw to stop the grumbling of disappointed committee members who realized despite the wonderful things it could do, there was no room in the budget for it.

"As director of sales and marketing at *Nest 2 Nest,* I am prepared to offer one time and one time only the following. First," he raised a finger, "no installation and equipment fee and," a second finger joined the first, "no maintenance fee for six months. However, if I leave the room without a signed contract, the deal is off the table."

Their grumbling turned to, "Wow, maybe we should get two."

Roscoe had seen it before. A salesman strolls into Abner with the latest and greatest, and the committee buys it hook, line, and sinker. He saw the way things were going and tried to head them off with, "I'll need time to read the fine print on the order form." The more he heard *of Nest 2 Nest* the more suspicious he became. "I have your card and will contact you if there are any questions."

"Are you out of your mind?" Ferrel asked as he threw an arm around JJ's shoulders. "Were you listening when he said it's a onetime offer? If he leaves without closing the deal, it's over. The nut has been found and guess what, your team lost. I'm no genius but I'm smart enough to know you can't beat free any day of the week." He looked around the table and nodded at Logan, a new member of the committee. It took a moment for him to figure out what Ferrel wanted then said, "I move we sign up with JJ and..."

JJ waved his paws, stopping him. "You don't sign up with me. You sign up with *Nest 2 Nest Communications,* a rock-solid organization that has weathered today's unpredictable economic climate. And, you sign with a company that is committed to GCS, Guaranteed Customer Satisfaction." When JJ finished, he grabbed Ferrel's paw and raised it in the air.

"Second," someone shouted.

Ferrel said, "All in favor say aye."

The committee responded with, "Aye," and were so excited about getting the system installed as quickly as possible they didn't hear Roscoe say, "Opposed." Along with objecting, he could have pointed out Ferrel isn't on the committee so he couldn't be part of the voting process but knew it wouldn't make any difference, someone would take his place.

"Shall we retire to *Out On A Limb* gentleman? Lunch is on me," JJ announced as he led Ferrel and the committee down the steps, and across the Clearing.

Roscoe remained seated at his desk while E.A. Poe removed the receiver from the conference table and put it and the Central Control Unit in a carrying case. "This is a demonstration model Mr. Chairman," he explained, "your equipment will arrive in a few days."

He closed the door leaving Roscoe alone, wondering what he could have done to have kept this from happening.

A few days after their first visit, J. Jay, and E.A. Poe returned with a new CCU and receiver. While E.A. Poe installed the equipment, JJ gave Roscoe and Megan a quick lesson on how to use it. When they finished, JJ wished them well and left.

Their departure was followed by a procession of community members who'd heard about the unit and wanted to see it for themselves. Several asked if they could use it to talk to a family member in another community. The room was so crowded and noisy, Roscoe decided to go to the library if he wanted to get something done.

The thing that bothered him was Sparky, the first person in the community to try a new technical device, had shown no interest in the unit. In fact, he urged Roscoe not to accept it when it was delivered or disconnect it after it was installed. When pressed for a reason, he shrugged and said, "If you don't know how something works you shouldn't use it." He added, "There's nothing wrong with the mail delivery system so why change it."

He asked Roscoe a technical question he couldn't answer and said, "I'm telling you Roscoe if you go through with this you're asking for trouble."

Roscoe explained his paws were tied, the committee had spoken and couldn't be prouder they'd embraced a new technology and in doing so had leaped over less adventurous communities.

The first time Roscoe received a message he looked for the manual to see what he was supposed to do. He pushed buttons on the receiver and said, "Hello," several times before remembering green was for talking, blue for listening.

"Roscoe," the voice on the other end of the line said. "This is Highly Exalted Chairman Cletus calling from COC headquarters. Can you hear me?"

Roscoe nodded, then realized Cletus couldn't see him. He pushed the green button on the receiver and said, "Loud and clear sir."

"The reason I'm calling is the Community of Clyde needs our help. Three days of rain sent a river near them over its banks wiping out trails and destroying the place where stored their winter food supply. It's not their fault, it's a case of being in the wrong place at the wrong time. Fortunately, no lives were lost." Roscoe sensed he was getting to the purpose of the call. "I am making a plea for every community in neighborhood seven to contribute seeds to help get them through this crisis."

"We'll do what we can. Is there anything..." Roscoe stopped; Cletus wasn't finished. "If you'll have someone bring the seeds to COC headquarters, we'll take them to Clyde. It will be more efficient coming from a central location. We're not sure if it's safe to go in, standing water could prevent us from getting there, but we have to try" There was a pause as he considered if what he was about to say would sound pushy. "They're desperate Roscoe. Can you get on this immediately?"

"I will sir," Roscoe said, but found he was speaking to air. "Hello?" he said but was too late, Cletus had signed off and was calling another community.

Marvin was chosen to be Abner's representative. He was given a sack of seeds, reminded of the urgency of his mission, and told not to get sidetracked on the way, the fate of a community depended on getting the seeds there on time. Then, with a wave of a paw and a promise to get to COC headquarters before dark, he took off to a chorus of cheers from the crowd gathered in the Clearing.

After he left, they stood around basking in the joy of helping a community in need. "It's the way things are supposed to work," they told each other. There was also the sense that, if they were in trouble, other communities would have their back.

"Roscoe," a voice called, and he couldn't tell if it was part of a dream, or someone actually saying his name. He opened one eye and found he was looking into the concerned face of Doug, the seed school custodian, and for the last few days, the meeting room.

"Doug?" Roscoe asked groggily. "What..."

"Sorry to bother you but the thing, the machine thing, is buzzing." Doug was afraid to say more, he didn't want to wake Penny Sue up.

"Buzzing?" Roscoe asked, not fully awake.

Doug nodded. "You know. The thing by your desk."

Roscoe sat up and felt for a slipper with his foot.

"And saying your name. I was putting cleaning supplies in the closet and..." Doug explained while helping Roscoe put on his robe.

"What time is it?" Roscoe asked.

"Late. I was cleaning the meeting room and didn't know what to do so I..."

"Let's go," Roscoe said and followed Doug over the edge of his nest and down the tree.

"...calling for Roscoe," the voice from the receiver said as they entered the meeting room.

When Roscoe answered, Cletus apologized for calling so late, then got to the point. "I was wondering if your courier left this afternoon or waiting until morning?" Disappointment could be heard in his voice he'd hoped to leave for Clyde at daybreak.

"He's not there?" Roscoe asked, then shook his head, he wouldn't be calling if he was. "What I mean is, he left yesterday afternoon, he should be there by now."

His comment was followed by a pause as Cletus asked if anyone had arrived since he'd been on the phone. Then he was back. "No one has seen him. Will you look into it and get back to me?"

"Yes sir, I will." Roscoe told him.

"Time is of the essence Mr. Chairman. The children in Clyde are starving." There it is Roscoe thought. Cletus knew how to motivate people. If changing the children were hungry to starving lit a fire under you, he didn't hesitate doing it.

Roscoe sat at his desk with his face in his paws, waiting for the safety team to arrive. He hadn't slept well to begin with, and knowing Marvin made a wrong turn and was wandering around in unfamiliar territory was going to keep him up a little longer.

Walking in the woods at night wasn't one of Roscoe's favorite things to do. The only consolation was he wasn't alone, the safety team and several committee members were with him. Two from the group had gone back to their nest with injuries. One after spraining an ankle when he stepped in a hole and the other to remove a thorn after walking into a rose bush.

Someone hollered, "Over here." As he ran toward the voice, Roscoe found himself thinking they should have sent someone else, Marvin was easily distracted. If the school Find The Nut team was practicing when he went by, he'd forget what he was doing and watch. Or if a friend said he was going to the bowling alley he'd go with him, the plight of the Community of Clyde forgotten.

What he didn't expect to find was a semi-conscious Marvin, tied to a tree. After untying him, Lester gave him a sip of walnut tea and he slowly came around. He shook his arms trying to get feeling back while members of the safety team asked what happened.

He told them, "I was on my way to COC headquarters when a stranger stopped me and asked how to get to Abner. I woke up tied to a tree with a knot on my head the size of a walnut and Lester asking me how many paws he was holding up."

Roscoe helped him to his feet and looked for the bag of seeds he was to deliver but couldn't find it. He knew it would do no good to ask Marvin where it was, he was still groggy from the blow to his head.

Since they were halfway to COC headquarters, Roscoe volunteered to deliver the bad news in person. He asked Lester to help Marvin get to his nest then call an emergency committee meeting for the first thing in the morning to go over the incident and find out what went wrong.

The next morning Roscoe was about to call the meeting to order when the receiver came to life and, after a blast of static he heard, "Roscoe? Chairman Ben here, can we talk?"

Roscoe pushed the green button, explained he was in a meeting and would call back when it was over.

Ben mumbled something Roscoe couldn't hear then speaking to the committee said, "Could we have the room? There's something I need to discuss with Roscoe of a, ah, sensitive nature."

Roscoe looked up and saw committee members had left their place at the conference table and were huddled around the receiver, listening to the conversation. "Guys," Roscoe said, and they reluctantly left the room. He closed the door, returned to his desk, picked up the receiver and said, "They're gone, you can speak freely."

Ben started to say something, stopped, gathered himself, and started over. "We took out a loan of several hundred seeds to provide health care services at the senior center." He paused, reluctant to go on. "I won't go into the details of the arrangement, but we're a few seeds short of a payment due tomorrow." He sighed and Roscoe could tell asking for help wasn't easy for him. "I'm calling to ask if we could borrow a dozen seeds to tide us over? We'll pay you back as soon as we receive the dividend from an investment we made."

"We'd be happy to help. I'll have it ready this afternoon. Is that soon enough?" Roscoe asked.

"I'll send Gaylord over to pick it up. He's empowered to sign whatever documents are required to release the seeds." Roscoe heard relief in Ben's voice and told him, "There's nothing to sign. You're a good neighbor, we trust you." He tried to sound upbeat, hoping to ease the embarrassment of asking for help.

Roscoe heard a muffled laugh. Apparently, Ben didn't because he continued like nothing happened. "Thanks Roscoe, I don't know what we would do if you..." The line went dead and after saying, "Hello," several times, Roscoe found he was holding the receiver, listening to static.

That afternoon Roscoe was about to put a document in the file cabinet when a stranger entered the room. He raised a paw when he saw Roscoe and said, "I'm here for the seeds Ben called about."

"You're Gaylord?" There was something about the stranger that bothered Roscoe. He knew most who lived in Ben but didn't recognize him.

"Who?" The stranger asked, regrouped and said, "Oh, Gaylord. Right."

"We have everything ready but there is the issue of the password." When he was talking to Ben, nothing was said about a password, but this would give him a chance to see how Gaylord or whoever he was, handled the situation.

The one who claimed to be Gaylord tapped his chin and looked around the room for a hint. He spotted the bag of seeds on Roscoe's desk, said, "Bailout?" and studied Roscoe's face to see if he was close.

"That seals the deal. Take the seeds and you're on your way," Roscoe said as he handed him the bag of seeds.

As the one who said he was Gaylord started down the path to Ben, Roscoe hurried to the safety training room and found Lester putting bandages on a shelf. He told him about his suspicion that Gaylord was a phony and asked him to follow him and see where he went. He was pretty sure he wasn't going to Ben. "Not too close. We don't know if he's doing this on his own or if others are involved. Remember what happened to Marvin."

Lester nodded and took off.

Roscoe entered the library, found Webster at the checkout desk, and said quietly, "I have a book request from Chairman Ben." Several community members were in the library, and he didn't want them to hear his suspicion that he'd sent a bag of seeds with an impostor.

Webster tapped a pencil on the desk, exhaled noisily, and said, "I don't believe he has a card with us." He opened the box containing cards with the names of library patrons, leafed through them and found it was as he thought. "I know he's a friend of yours but it's against library policy to loan books to non-card holders."

Roscoe wasn't expecting this. He needed to get a message to Ben as fast as possible and sending a note in a book seemed the best way to do it. He hadn't counted on running into library red tape. "Check it out on my card?" he said, wanting to move things along.

Webster frowned. This was the kind of thing that drove him crazy. If Roscoe had checked the book out and taken it to Ben he could live with it. But to check it out now, knowing it would leave the community and end up who knows where went against library policy. "What's the title of the book?" he asked when he saw the look of frustration on Roscoe's face.

"What would you suggest?" Roscoe didn't care which book he selected as long as it was big enough to put a note inside.

Webster looked puzzled. "I don't understand. You said Ben requested a book, now you're asking me to pick one for him? What are you guys doing, passing notes during third hour at seed school?" He meant it as a joke and was caught off guard when Roscoe grabbed his arm and said through clenched teeth, "The workroom. Now."

"Look Roscoe. If you want to take a book to your friend, do it but you have to realize there are rules ..." Webster stopped when Roscoe pushed him against the wall and said, "There are things going on you're not aware of and I don't have time to explain. You'll have to trust me."

Webster couldn't remember Roscoe acting like this. He raised his paws and said, "Sure. No problem. I'll get a book you can take to..." He stopped when Roscoe shook his head and asked, "What?"

"I'm not taking it, you are." Roscoe leaned on the worktable and explained, "If they see me anywhere near the Community of Ben it's over."

"Who'll see you? What's over?" Webster asked as he worked his way to the door. He wasn't sure if Roscoe heard him, he was busy writing something on the back of an overdue book notice.

"I'll get a book. A mystery or ..." When Webster opened the door, he found he was looking into the faces of library patrons who, moments before, were milling around, trying to find something to read. When they saw Roscoe shove Webster into the workroom, they wondered what was going on.

"And" Webster was not at his best in situations like this, "when you finish, leave it on my desk." He turned to the crowd by the door and explained, "He's filling out an application for employment. Here. At the library. With me."

"Oh," several said. "I see," from others. As they went back to what they were doing they wondered why Roscoe needed another job. Wasn't he's always complaining about not having time to get things done?

Roscoe followed Webster out of the workroom, pulled a book from a shelf, stuck a note inside, shoved it toward him and said, "Take this to Ben."

Webster glanced at the title and almost refused to take it when he saw, *The Curious Case of the Missing Delivery Boy* by Leland Waffle. He was going to get another book, maybe something from the children's section about a hamster and parakeet who become friends at a pet store but didn't when he saw Roscoe standing by the door, tapping his foot, and gesturing for him to get on with it, he hadn't a moment to lose.

"I'm not built for this," Webster grumbled as he walked to the big rock that separates Abner from Ben. "I was meant to spend my days in the library arranging books and finding reference material for students." The library was his home, his sanctuary. He'd been there long enough to know the location of every loose floorboard

143

and sagging bookshelf. He'd only been past the big rock once when he helped Roscoe get a message to a small human named Sammy.

He was trying to figure out which path took him to Ben when a heavyset guy wearing a plaid vest, stepped from behind the rock and asked, "You lost?"

Webster shrugged thinking lost was a relative term. He knew where he was going but wasn't sure how to get there.

"Is that a yes, or no?" The stranger asked as an accomplice snuck behind Webster, lifted him off his feet, and carried him to the other side of the rock so they wouldn't be seen by someone passing by.

When the stranger put him down, Webster looked around and was amazed at the radio equipment he saw under a makeshift canopy. An operator, wearing headphones was sitting at a table, listening to communication between Ben and Abner.

"Kind of far from your dinky little library, aren't you?" The guy in the vest asked.

"Book," Webster managed to say. "Delivery." He held up the book Roscoe gave him. The stranger grabbed it, chuckled when he read the title, and slammed the book against Webster's chest. "Your creepy little helpers take care of things like this, why are you delivering it?"

Don't respond, Webster told himself. You're a prisoner being held against your will. He wants you to get angry and say something stupid but keeping quiet wasn't easy. His library wasn't dinky, and his helpers were far from creepy, they were the smartest students in seed school. They had to be to work there.

The stranger started to say something else but stopped when the one at the radio said, "I got something JJ." He leaned forward, straining to hear what was said. He slid the headphones off. "He's legit. Roscoe asked Ben if he got the book he sent."

JJ thought about the conversation between chairman, turned to ask his captive a question, and discovered he was gone. He snapped his fingers to get E.A. Poe's attention, then ran to the side of the rock where he met Webster earlier, but he wasn't there. "Spread out guys. E.A. go to Abner. I'll follow the path to Ben. Stewie, stay on the radio. That four eyed weasel can't have gone far."

When he thought it was safe, Webster crawled down from the top of the big rock. He was sure one of them would look up and see him but in their hurry to catch him before reaching Ben, they hadn't. He took a shortcut back to the Abner. He was on his turf now, jogging through woods he knew like the inside of the library.

"Can you help me?" Roscoe hated to interrupt but from his perspective, Sparky wasn't doing anything important. He'd carried the central control unit to his lab but after removing it from the case and putting it on the workbench, Sparky hadn't looked at it.

"I told you, you have to understand the technology before using it. And you bring this," he poked the CCU with a paw, "piece of junk to the lab and expect me to do something with it?" Roscoe was surprised by his angry response to a simple question. He was usually curious about anything of a technical nature, but the moment he put the unit on the worktable, Sparky turned away and became involved in arranging his collection of screwdrivers by size.

"Look," he said after slamming a screwdriver on the worktable, "the unit sends a signal through the air. Okay? Anyone with a receiver tuned to the same frequency can listen in. It's that simple." He spun around and walked to the unit. "It's a kit for goodness sake. They're cheap, you can buy one anywhere." He tugged on the *Nest 2 Nest* logo stuck to the side of the case. It came off revealing a sticker for a company named *InterNest*. Beneath it was another one that said it was *HoMade Kit Model 19B*.

Sparky gave the stickers he'd removed to Roscoe and had an, I told you so, look on his face. "The parts are cheap, okay? The circuitry is clipped together, not soldered." He poked inside the unit with a finger. "It's laughable. It's a joke." He looked closer and grew quiet. Roscoe heard him mumble something about removing a relay and adding a feedback loop. Nothing he said made sense to him.

It wasn't long before Sparky produced a soldering iron and a box of electronic parts. He stepped back once, shook his head and mumbled, "Not there. Maybe here." Then he was back at work, removing existing parts and replacing them with new ones.

Roscoe loved to watch Sparky work. His concentration was such that he could leave, come back in the morning, and Sparky wouldn't know he'd gone.

Finally, he straightened and said with disgust. "Give that a try." He walked to a small sink and washed his paws an act Roscoe took to mean he was sorry he'd touched the cheap piece of junk.

"Help me out Sparks, give what a try?" Roscoe hated to push him considering the mood he was in but if he didn't, Sparky would start working on something and assume since he'd watched what he was doing, he understood what was going on.

He didn't.

Sparky stood at the sink and mumbled, "Okay. I reconfigured the distribution circuits and replaced the audio output relay."

"Which means?"

"You say hello. Whoever is listening hears, hello, hello, hello. It's called the echo effect. Pretty basic stuff."

For you, Roscoe wanted to say but didn't, Sparky was upset enough already. He hadn't followed everything he said but caught that he'd changed something in the central control unit and whoever was listening would come to the meeting room to fix what had gone wrong with the equipment.

"If it's not too personal, why are you so upset about this?" Roscoe asked, puzzled by his indifference.

Sparky shrugged. "It's my idea. I was a first year in seed school and sent sketches of my design to a magazine. I didn't hear back from them and thought they rejected my idea. Then this thing shows up." He sighed. "I was young and thought everyone played by the rules." He finished with both paws on the workbench, staring at a roll of duct tape.

Roscoe smiled, put a paw on his shoulder and asked, "You ready for a little payback?"

Roscoe was in the meeting room. The central control unit was on the floor next to his desk. Before placing the call, he'd asked Sparky if he was sure it would work like he said it would. He gave Roscoe a look that said, you're kidding, right?" He held the green button down and said, "Chairman Ben. This is Roscoe calling."

Under the tent near the big rock Stewie sat up and pressed the headset to his ears. Something was wrong but he needed to hear more before telling JJ about it. He lifted his pencil and prepared to write what he heard. "This this is this, is is Roscoe, Rosc Rosc called calling." The rest was garbled. Words were out of order and didn't make sense. Something in the CCU had broken or was about to, he didn't know. He was a radio operator not a repairman, that was E. A. Poe's job.

Roscoe, Sparky, and the safety team sat around the conference table in the dark. They'd been there since sundown and to Roscoe's surprise, no one had said a word. He thought of calling things off when a storm swept through the area and although brief, was intense. It was still drizzling but nothing like when the front passed through. He doubted anyone would be checking on electronic equipment in conditions like this.

He was about to tell them to go home, they'd try again tomorrow night, when he heard footsteps on the platform outside the room. The door opened and two figures, dressed in black stepped inside. "The CCU is next to the desk," JJ whispered to E.A. Poe.

E.A. Poe tiptoed across the room and said, "Found it."

Matches were struck and touched to the wick of the candles held in the paws of those around the table.

Roscoe told him to, "Take the unit, we don't want it."

Ever the salesman, JJ recovered quickly. "This is a routine maintenance call Mr. Chairman. It's in the contract you signed. There won't be a charge."

"At night? In a rainstorm?" Roscoe asked as he crossed the room and placed a candle on his desk.

"Like I said in my presentation, *Nest 2 Nest* is on the job twenty-four seven," JJ answered in a surprisingly calm voice given the awkward situation he was in.

"You stole my work!" Sparky shouted and would have left his place at the table if Lester hadn't grabbed his arm and told him to settle down, let Roscoe handle it.

"Who's he?" JJ asked as he lifted a paw to his forehead, staring into the dark room.

Before Roscoe could answer the door flew open and a thoroughly drenched Webster entered. He held a rain-soaked book in his paw, shook it in JJ's face and said, "You owe me buster, this book is ruined."

That was enough for JJ. He saw an opening between Webster and the door and, moving at surprising speed for someone his size, ran through it. When he reached the platform, he found Chairman Ben standing at the foot of the stairs daring him to try and get by. He grabbed the handrail, vaulted over the side, and discovered why the platform was there. After a rain of any size, sprinkle or downpour, puddles formed and the ground around the meeting room stayed wet for days.

Standing in mud up to his knees, he prepared for the worst.

"JJ? Is that you?" Ferrel's voice cut through the darkness. He hadn't been included in the stakeout because Roscoe knew he couldn't keep quiet if his life depended on it.

He was on his way home from the bowling alley when he saw JJ standing in a puddle of mud. He grabbed his paw, helped him to dry ground and said, "You'll be coming to Abner often so you should use the stairs in weather like this."

He put a paw on JJ's shoulder and said, "Years ago, there was a community member named Ellis, but everyone called High Water because every time it rained..." Ferrel started on his collection of stories of others who'd found themselves in the same situation JJ was in, up to their knees in mud.

As they walked away, JJ looked at Roscoe and gave him a look that said, "Help me. Please."

"Say," Ferrel stopped in the middle of another story about Ellis, "you don't have one of those coupons for *Out On A Limb*, do you?" Then he returned to his story. "So, one-night, High Water was on his way home from visiting a friend, and it started..."

Roscoe had tried to think of a way to punish JJ for the scam he pulled on the community. He was sure they'd get their seeds back. E.A. Poe would tell the safety team what they wanted to know in exchange for not including his name in their report to the COC.

He called JJ back to the meeting room. He wanted him to suffer for what he'd done but allowing Ferrel to go on much longer would be considered cruel and unusual punishment. He wouldn't wish that on anyone, not even a scoundrel like JJ.

BIG G MINI AND THE BATTLE
AT LITTLE SANDY

Harold pulled into *The Big G Grocery and Otis Tharp Fountain Pen Museum* parking lot and found a pickup truck for *Leon Surveys* in his reserved space. As he walked to the backdoor of the museum, he saw men working in the field between the parking lot and the woods. He was trying to figure out what was going on when the door opened and Dawson said, "Step on it, Big G is waiting."

"For what? I didn't get a memo about a meeting," Harold said defensively.

Dawson shook his head and asked, "Did you check the calendar on your phone?"

"My secretary kept track of my schedule before Big G fired her." Harold didn't know how things on his phone worked, he seldom used it.

"Give it to me," Dawson said and waited impatiently for Harold to remove the phone from his briefcase and hand it to him. He pressed a few buttons, turned it off and back on, gave it back and said, "There you go."

Harold looked and saw on today's page of his calendar; a meeting was scheduled for eight o'clock in the security room.

On their way to his office Harold told Dawson, "I'd be more helpful if I knew the subject of the meeting and had a chance to prepare."

"You don't get it do you? Big G wants your gut response not a well thought out answer," Dawson explained as he made a shooing motion with his hands, encouraging Harold to get moving or they'd be late for the meeting.

That was another thing that bothered Harold. Why meet in the security room? It wasn't much larger than a closet. With a locker at one end and security monitors covering an entire wall, there was barely room for Officer Gardner and him.

When he arrived, the room was filled with managers from Big G's stores, plus someone he didn't recognize. Big G glanced at his watch and grunted, "Good you could join us Finebender. Talk about a penny holding up a dime."

The managers snickered at the comment. One reached behind Harold and closed the door.

Big G addressed the group. "I know you're busy with plenty of work on your plate, but I want you to hear it from me before you read about it in the newspaper." He waited a moment before saying, "Hogan, Snead, and Old Tom Morris," then looked for raised hands from managers eager to impress him by identifying the names he mentioned. Instead, he got blank looks and comments mumbled so quietly he could barely hear them. Finally, one of the managers asked, "Is Old Tom Morris a soft drink?"

"Finebender," Big G bellowed, ignoring the manager's questions.

"Yes," Harold said.

"Do those names mean anything to you?"

"Actually, they do. They are famous golfers. In fact, the pen Old Tom Morris used to sign..."

"They. Are. Golfers." Big G repeated slowly in case the managers didn't hear Harold's answer. He raised his eyebrows, expecting someone to ask what they had to do with the grocery business. When no one did, he turned to the stranger and said, "You want to fill them in Leon?"

The stranger stood and Harold saw *Leon Surveys* printed above the pocket of his denim shirt. He was shorter than Big G, skinny as a rail, and permanently tanned from spending a lifetime outdoors. Sunglasses were perched on the bill of his ball cap. "While we are meeting in here my men, using high tech surveying equipment, are defining the contour of the field you see here." He pointed to a monitor that showed the field crawling with workers.

"Why?" Harold asked.

Leon looked at Big G, not sure where the technical part of the meeting stopped and the reason he was there started. Big G glared at Harold before saying, "I thought a smart guy like you would have figured it out by now."

"It has something to do with golf, but the field isn't large enough for one hole. It would have to be a short one. A par three."

"Once again Finbender you're close but get no cigar." He looked around, spotted Dawson and asked, "Where'd he go wrong?"

Dawson looked at Harold for a hint. When he didn't get one, he said, "Par four?"

"Think smaller," from Big G.

Dawson offered a hesitant, "Two?"

Big G pulled the stub of a cigar from his mouth and slammed it in the wastebasket by Harold's desk to show his disgust with the answer. "When I said smaller, I meant real small. Like miniature golf."

"Of course." "That will work." "Excellent idea." From the managers.

To help them visualize what he was talking about, Big G lifted a piece of cardboard hidden behind Harold's desk and turned it around. They saw *Layout of the Big G Miniature Golf Course* written across the bottom with a marker. Holes crisscrossed the field, covering every inch of space. Harold saw a windmill on one fairway and a clown on another. One hole started at the edge of the field, made a half circle through the woods, and ended back where it started. Next to it Big G had written *Bonus Hole? Free groceries for a hole in one?* with a blue marker.

When the meeting was over the managers left the room, talking excitedly about Big G's plan and the part they'd play in making it happen. Harold went to his desk and was about to sit down when a familiar voice said, "Morning boss."

He looked up and saw Baylor Reed, a former volunteer at the museum standing in the doorway. He taught history at the Centerline High School for thirty-five years, was a frequent visitor to the museum, and became a tour guide when he retired. He added background information on fountain pens other volunteers didn't know. It wasn't unusual for visitors to wait until he was available to go on a tour. He quit when Big G became the owner of the building and insisted volunteers, "Learn the grocery business, or take a hike." Baylor told Harold he didn't need the aggravation and quit.

After taking a few minutes to catch up Harold asked, "What brings you downtown?"

"I'm on my way to city hall to get a permit for an event we're planning. Since it's on the way, I thought I'd drop by and say hello."

"Does it have anything to do with your civil war group?" Harold asked, intrigued.

"We're reenactors. Our unit is called *The River Rats*," Baylor said proudly.

Harold thought about what he said before asking, "Where did a name like that come from? There isn't a river in this part of the city."

"Not now, but there was a hundred and fifty years ago. In fact, the Little Sandy ran across the field behind the museum and ended at the pond in the woods. In the thirties the Corps of Engineers rerouted it so the city could develop property in the area."

Harold tried to picture what it would have looked like. Other than the pond in the woods, there was nothing to suggest a river crossed the field. There was also something he said about city hall that stuck in the back of his mind.

"Actually, a major skirmish was fought here," Baylor said. "The history books call it *The Battle at Little Sandy*. I'm surprised you haven't heard of it."

Harold knew it wouldn't be long before Big G sent Dawson to find out who the visitor was, so he asked, "Have you seen the pen from Galvonia? It's across the hall." While they walked to the room, Harold lowered his voice and said, "Have the battle here, in the field behind the museum."

While Baylor considered the suggestion, Dawson entered the room and said, "I don't believe I've met your guest."

"This is Baylor Reed; he was a volunteer at the museum before Big G bought it. He's a retired teacher, read about the pen from Galvonia, and stopped by to see it."

"Really?" Dawson said skeptically. "And you have to whisper to do that?"

"It's how Mr. Finebender trained us," Baylor said with a smile. "That way we didn't bother another group if we were in the same room. Old habits die hard," he said with a chuckle.

Dawson considered his answer, then hurried out of the room. Harold was sure he was on his way to Big G's office to report what he'd learned.

Harold opened the front door of the museum, shook Baylor's hand and said, "If you have the battle here, I'll feature pens from that era. When the tour is over, we'll go outside and watch the *River Rats* perform. I'll build a program around it."

"That's a great idea. With the museum behind it we're sure to get a big crowd," Baylor said as ran to catch the bus before it pulled away from the curb.

Harold stood on the steps in front of the museum thinking the skirmish at Little Sandy wasn't the only battle that would be fought that day.

A few days after Baylor's visit, Harold knocked on the door to Dawson's office and asked if he wanted to go to lunch. The idea came to him while on his way to work. Vinny Bling had connections at city hall and with a word to the right person, Big G's request for a permit to build a miniature golf course would end up in a cardboard box in the basement, gathering dust. That would open the way for Baylor Reed to stage *The Battle at Little Sandy*, protect the squirrels from losing part of the woods and keep them from having to deal with lights and the noise of golfers late at the night.

Dawson became uneasy when he saw the part of town where Harold was taking him. Sensing his discomfort Harold said, "It's a little rough around the edges but it's worth it, Rosie's pizza sauce is the best in Centerline."

When they entered the restaurant, Harold was encouraged when he saw Bruno and Vinny in their usual booth, their heads almost touching, talking quietly.

As Rosie took them to a booth away from Vinny's, Harold whispered, "I was hoping to be close enough for Vinny to hear our conversation." After seating them near the front window, Rosie gave them each a menu and took their drink order. Nothing in his manner suggested he heard what Harold said.

They made small talk while they waited for their lunch to arrive. A waiter brought their drinks but before leaving, replaced the saltshaker on the table with a new one. He saw the confused look on Dawson's face, the shaker he replaced had plenty of salt in it. He explained, "There's a lot of moisture in the air this time of year. Rising pizza dough, water boiling on the stove for pasta, and the front door opening, and closing lets in humidity. The salt clumps together and won't come out of the shaker." After receiving a, who cares shrug from Dawson, the waiter winked at Harold and walked away.

While they ate Harold asked how the permit for the miniature golf course was coming along.

"It's on the commissioner's desk waiting for her signature. When she signs it, we're good to go," Dawson told him with an air of confidence,

"Does the permit have a name or number?" Harold asked, trying to sound like he was making conversation until their pizza arrived.

Dawson looked around to make sure no one was listening before whispering, "BG Mini P247." He wanted Harold to know he was privy to information the other managers weren't. Besides, the place was practically empty, who would hear?

Harold asked if he'd ever seen a historical reenactment. Dawson shook his head and mumbled, "Who has time?" before taking a bite of pizza.

Harold mentioned his friend Baylor Reed filed a request to reenact a battle that took place in the field behind the museum. "Good luck with that," Dawson said with a laugh. "Big G says the miniature golf course is a done deal."

Harold was relieved when he saw Bruno leave his booth and head for the door.

Rosie asked if they wanted dessert. Dawson waved him off, saying he had a ton of work to do before construction on the miniature golf course started. Harold took the bill from Rosie and told Dawson since he'd invited him, he'd pay for both.

As they walked by his booth Vinny mumbled, "Bruno's on it."

On the way to Harold's car, Dawson asked what the guy in the pin stripped suit said.

Harold told him, "Buena sera. I think it's Italian for good afternoon or evening. He says it to everyone." As he pulled away from the curb, he noticed the men who stood near the entrance to Rosie's were gone.

It had been two weeks and Big G was getting nervous. He hadn't heard from Commissioner Feebly who promised the project was a shoo-in, a slam dunk, a no brainer. When he called, the commissioner's secretary said she was visiting a construction site and didn't know when she'd return.

Calling city hall to find out what was holding things up ended in frustration. Like now. He was on hold with the third employee he'd talked to. He'd been to *Permit Receiving,* (Yes, they'd received it), and *Permit Processing,* (Yes it had been processed). He'd been waiting ten minutes for an employee in the *Permit Approval* department to return.

"Hello?" A voice different than the person he was talking to said.

"Yes," Big G glanced at his notepad, "Teresa. Were you able to find..."

"Teresa went to lunch. I'm Sonia, how can I help?" the voice on the phone asked.

He slammed the phone on the receiver and shouted in frustration. He'd been on the phone thirty minutes and hadn't accomplished a thing. He pulled a cigar from a humidor in a drawer in his desk and walked to the window. He almost dropped the cigar when he saw a platoon of men in blue uniforms, led by a boy beating a drum, turn off the street in front of the museum, and march across the parking lot. They were followed by a horse pulling a covered wagon with pots and pans hanging from hooks on the side.

He was sure they'd stop when they reached edge of the parking lot and saw the rows of yellow flags in the field marking the location of fairways and greens put there by Leon's surveyors. It had cost a bundle to get this far.

The soldiers kept going, stepping on flags, and erasing chalk marks as they marched to the middle of the field.

"No! No! No!" he screamed at the window, hit a button on his phone and shouted, "Dawson! My office! Now!"

Nadine had the dusk to midnight watch at the edge of the woods. Her being there represented a victory for the females in Abner. *The Committee for the Protection of Neighborhood Resources* dug in their heels and refused to allow females to stand guard saying it was physically demanding and required a discipline to rigorous for their sensitive nature to handle. They argued females didn't have the stamina required to stay alert during a shift at night. And, if there was a danger to the community, they doubted they could shout loud enough for their warning to be heard.

The females fought back, insisting if someone like Pomeroy, a seed school dropout who couldn't hold a steady job and hung out at the bowling alley until it closed could stand guard, they were more than capable of doing it. Tension in the community grew as meals were late, beds went unmade, and holes in caps worn on the heads of committee members on cold nights went unmended.

The committee relented, allowing them to stand guard during the day. When they proved capable of handling that, they were assigned to the night watch.

Nadine didn't understand what was going on in the field. Humans sat around campfires cleaning equipment and talking quietly to one another.

They were building something where Seed Man parked his car, but she had no idea what it was.

All activity stopped when a human walked to the middle of the field and played a song on a musical instrument. As the last note faded away, everyone picked up what they'd been working on, went to their tents, and grew quiet.

A human she guessed was a guard like her, walked around the camp, keeping watch.

Just before her shift ended fog rolled in, muffling the sound of voices and shuffling feet in another part of the field. She reported this to Dewey her replacement for the midnight to dawn watch, who passed it on to Chloe who took over at daybreak.

When the sun rose high enough to burn away the fog, the *River Rats* were surprised to find they were facing a dozen Big G managers in the white shirts, ties, and slacks they wore to work the day before. When Big G ordered them to the field to protect the miniature golf course, they grabbed whatever weapons they could find on their desks. Several picked up staplers, a few grabbed tape dispensers. Others held their mobile phones in front of them, using them as shields.

Big G stood behind them, shouting instructions and moving them from one side of the field to the other. He wore an apron he'd grabbed from the grocery store in the museum auditorium and waved an unlit cigar.

The *River Rats* gathered around a map spread on a table and listened intently as Gunnery Sergeant Baylor Reed went over the plan of attack.

Ferrel leaned against a tree at the edge of the woods taking it all in. When he got there the fog was so thick, he couldn't see his paw in front of his face. As it slowly lifted, it reminded him of the fog machine his manager Rex used at the start of a concert. He saw humans sitting in temporary bleachers on the other side of the field.

A small human in a blue uniform beat a drum, slowly at first, then gradually picked up speed. An older human lifted an instrument to his mouth and played an upbeat tune.

The temptation proved too much. Ferrel left safety of the woods, dashed across the field and when he reached the bleachers, he was no longer Ferrel, ordinary member of a community of squirrels but FeRoll, the rapper.

He stopped in front of the bleachers and struck the pose his fans would recognize; head down, one leg forward like he was taking a step, and a paw thrust in the air.

He held the pose and was about to start his most popular song, *Don't Put That In My Nest*. There was an explosion and he jumped with surprise when a mound of dirt near his foot shot in the air. Another object whizzed over his head as he sprinted to the dumpster and dove beneath it.

The second shot was followed by whoops and cries as the *River Rats*, with the bayonets on their rifles gleaming, marched toward Big G and his managers. When they saw the wave of soldiers moving toward them, they realized the staplers and tape dispensers they were holding would only be effective if the battle involved paperwork. They dropped their weapons and raised their arms in surrender.

Baylor Reed had almost reached Big G when he heard horse hooves and the sound of pots and pans banging together. He turned and saw Dawson driving the covered wagon across the field. He dove to get out of the way as the wheels of the wagon passed within inches of his highly polished boots.

Dawson stopped long enough for Big G to climb on, then continued across the parking lot and into the street. Horns honked and drivers slammed on their breaks to avoid hitting the wagon as it sped away from the battlefield.

The crowd on the bleachers cheered thinking the dramatic escape was how *The Battle At Little Sandy* ended.

Baylor Reed watched them go and hoped they'd return soon; he promised to have the horse back at the stable before dark.

Ferrel stayed beneath the dumpster until the humans were gone. He crawled out, listening for sounds of danger. Hearing none, he jogged across the field and was challenged by Chloe who shouted, "Halt! Who goes there?"

"It's me," Ferrel said without slowing down. He was a community leader for heaven's sake, everyone knew him.

"Sorry Me but unless you say the password you can't enter the woods," Chloe said with a firmness that surprised him.

"Give it a rest," Ferrel said angrily. "I know community members in high places. When they hear that you…" The next thing he knew he was on the ground with Chloe's knee in his back.

"Good news wise guy," she whispered in his ear as she tied his paws together, "you'll be seeing your friends in high places real soon." She pulled him to his feet and told him to, "Start walking and don't try any funny stuff."

The next morning Harold slowed when he pulled in the parking lot and saw the covered wagon in his reserved place. He pulled alongside it, got out, and saw Dawson with the reins in his hands. Big G sat beside him, staring at the field. The horse that brought them there grazed in the grass near the dumpster.

He saw ruts made by the wagon wheels when they left the field, and chunks of turf turned over where the *River Rats* set up camp. A single flag placed by the surveyors where the bonus hole entered the woods, was all that remained of the *Big G Miniature Golf Course.*

He heard Big G mutter, "It's the woods, Dawson. It has to be the woods." He started to ask if they needed help, but Dawson shook his head and whispered, "Not now."

He walked to the backdoor, entered the code in the keypad and after a trip to Penultimate, went to his desk in the security room where he and Officer Gardner drank coffee and watched the monitor that showed the covered wagon in the parking lot.

Officer Gardner told Harold he should call 911 and report an unregistered vehicle was parked behind the museum. He took a sip of coffee and decided to wait a little longer, Big G wasn't going anywhere.

A NOTE ON THE MEETING ROOM FLOOR

It had been a typical end of the year meeting for the *Committee for the Protection of Neighborhood Resources*, wrapping up old business so they could start the new year with a clean slate. The only reason they met was because it was on the calendar. Several stayed home knowing there wasn't anything on the agenda that required a vote. The meeting finished early and following a long-standing tradition, they adjourned to *Out On A Limb* for walnut tea and nut cake to celebrate another year of balancing the books and keeping the community running smoothly.

Roscoe dropped a copy of the meeting minutes in Megan's in-box and was putting chairs around the conference table when he saw a crumpled piece of paper on the floor near the waste basket. He picked it up and was about to throw it away when he saw the word, "Leave," written in a corner.

His curiosity aroused, he opened it to see what else was written there. It looked like whoever left the note made several attempts to get the wording right. Apparently, none carried the impact the author hoped to convey because a line was drawn through each attempt. The thing that concerned him was the intensity of the message that ranged from, "Leave the community if you know what's good for you," to, "Leave now or suffer the consequences."

His first thought was whoever wrote the note meant it for him, though no names were mentioned. To make matters worse, he didn't know if it was written by someone on the committee or a previous meeting, he'd had several that day.

He tried to remember who attended the other meetings and decided to check his notes, he made a habit of keeping a list of those who attend. He was halfway to the file cabinet when the door opened, and Jarvis walked in. When he saw Roscoe, he gave a surprised, "Oh!" Then, "I thought the room was..."

"Is there something..." Roscoe asked, equally surprised, he thought the committee was at *Out On A Limb*.

"No. I was just, um, I mean..." Jarvis stammered as he looked around, trying to come up with a reason for being there.

"Did you..." Before Roscoe could ask if he had a question about a decision the committee made, Jarvis said, "There it is," crossed the room, lifted a hat off the hook near the door, put it on, apologized for stopping by so late and left.

His encounter with Jarvis didn't make sense. He'd obviously been looking for something other than the hat, it had been there for weeks. And when he put it on, it slipped over his ears, covering his eyes.

His appearance raised two questions for Roscoe. Did Jarvis write the note and come back to get it? Or did he receive it? And, if he received it, why didn't whoever sent it give him a clean copy with a single demand to leave, not a half dozen?

It was late so Roscoe put the note in the top drawer of his desk planning to look into it after the holidays. He blew out the candle and turned toward the door when someone jumped out of the utility closet and hit him on the head with a blunt instrument knocking him to the floor. The last thing he heard before losing consciousness was the sound of footsteps leaving the room.

When he came to, he was looking into the concerned face of Doug, the custodian, and members of the safety team.

As his vision cleared, he saw the room had been ransacked. Folders were pulled from the file cabinet and thrown on the floor. The drawers of his desk had been emptied and tossed in a corner of the room. Lester asked what happened and Roscoe said he didn't know. He was going to mention finding the note when the door opened and Leander, secretary to the Highly Exalted Chairman of the Committee of Committees, entered. He said something to the safety team who nodded and left. When he reached Lester, he asked if he could have a moment alone with Roscoe. Lester made sure Roscoe was okay and told him he'd be on the platform if he needed him.

After he left, Leander helped Roscoe to a chair and started with an apology. "You weren't supposed to find the note, it was left by accident. Then, to cover his tracks, the one who wrote it returned, attacked you, and trashed your office to make it look like a robbery. It was a foolish mistake and will result in the immediate termination of the agent involved."

Roscoe, still woozy from the blow to his head, had no idea what he was talking about. "An agent? Here? In Abner?"

Leander nodded. "There are no signs. Nothing to distinguish Abner from Ben."

"So, the agent was supposed to go to the Community of Ben?" Roscoe asked, trying to follow what he was saying.

Leander studied his paws, not sure how much he should say about *Operation Nightshade.*

"Why?" Roscoe asked. He couldn't think of a reason for an agent to be in either community.

Leander fiddled with the handle of his briefcase before saying, "You're making this very difficult. I admire what you've accomplished as committee chairman and consider you a friend, but I'm prevented by Article 5 of the Community Secrecy Act from saying more." He walked to the window above the wooden bench, looked out, and saw clusters of community members in the Clearing, talking to one another and pointing toward the meeting room. He shook his head knowing with a little care, this could have been avoided.

He returned, sat down next to Roscoe and said, "Documents were taken from my office at COC headquarters. Vital information intended for the highly exalted chairman's eyes only." He raised his paws in frustration. "Until the culprit is found, and the information returned, the stability of every community in neighborhood seven is at risk."

"There was nothing about that in the note I found." Roscoe tried to remember what it said. Someone should leave or was leaving? "It wasn't even a note, it looked like the writer was trying to decide what to say. Words were crossed out and others added. It didn't make sense."

"Not to the untrained eye," Leander said and decided Roscoe needed to see the bigger picture to understand what he was dealing with. He removed a secrecy agreement form from his briefcase, laid it on the conference table, and told Roscoe to sign next to the X at the bottom of the page.

"What is it?" Roscoe was not in the habit of signing something without reading it first.

"You'll have to trust me on this," Leander said and handed him a pencil. After signing the form, Leander stuck it in his briefcase, turned to him and asked. "You're familiar with FB4J?"

Roscoe nodded. He'd learned about the organization when the community was under attack by a group of small humans with BB guns. It stood for *Fight Back For Justice*.

Leander continued. "What looks to the casual observer like a clumsy attempt to compose a threatening message, is actually an encrypted document of the highest importance. It makes the connection between the break-in at the COC and someone living in Abner."

"How did it end up here? On the meeting room floor?" Roscoe asked, trying to make sense of what he heard.

Leander shook his head, he didn't know. "Agent Pond is missing. We think he was the mastermind behind the break in. Or, he may have gone the way of all squirrels attempting to stop the burglary." He paused, searching for words to explain the significance of what happened. "There are people in the criminal world who would pay a hefty price for the information on the documents that were taken."

"What could be so important?" Roscoe asked, thinking of the forms he filled out each year for the COC. The questions were general in nature. How many committee meetings in the past year? How many students in seed school? Is the safety team up to date on first aide qualifications?

"Community data. Intimate details of the lives of community members. The location of acorn storage units. Mailbox numbers.

Academic records from seed school." Leander raised his paws and sighed, "Everything a community member would want kept secret."

"What should we do?" Roscoe finally grasped the dangerous situation the community was in.

"At your next committee meeting ask the members to update their personal information. Issue new nest numbers. Let the manager of the post office and the principal of seed school know what's going on. The entire system has been compromised. There must be a complete reconstruction of every record on file at the time of the break in. When you finish, turn the information over to me and I'll get it back where it belongs."

Roscoe groaned as he thought of the committee's response to what Leander wanted. The reason there were no signs to help visitors find their way to Abner was because they couldn't agree on where to put them. Or what to put on them. Or if they were needed. They'd been working on the problem since they moved to the woods and were no closer to a decision than when they started. If they couldn't agree on something as simple as the location of a sign, how would they handle a problem as complicated as this?

Beck finished her last class before winter break. It marked the end of her first semester teaching in Abner and felt pretty good about it. There were the usual first days of hazing by the students, but it didn't take long for them to realize she was smart and, unlike some of their teachers, approachable. She was cleaning the chalkboard when she saw **JR © Ms. R** written in a corner. She erased it quickly, thought of JR, and wondered what he was doing.

On the way to her nest, she decided to stop by the lab. She opened the door, went inside, and saw him standing in front of a chalkboard, studying a column of numbers. She put her arms around him and whispered, "Surprise." It turned out the surprise was on her because when the person turned around, she had no idea who it was. She blushed, stepped back, and stammered, "I'm sorry. I thought you were…"

The person smiled, stuck out a paw and said, "I'm Sparky. You must be Rebecca. JR told me about you."

Beck had two thoughts, neither of them good. The first was, although she'd dreamed of meeting Sparky since she was a student in seed school, she hadn't pictured it happening like this. The second was, if Sparky was back, where was JR? Did he return to the science academy without saying goodbye?

She missed it the first time Sparky said it, so he repeated, "He's at the library doing research for his book." She was almost to the door when he told her, "He plans to stay in Abner for the holidays."

She entered the library and looked around but didn't see him. She guessed things slowed down over the holidays because other than two boys looking at books by Coach Bobby on the fundamentals of find the nut, it was empty. She started to go but stopped when JR left the Science and Technology section with a stack of books.

She waited until he was almost to her before saying, "Hey handsome." She closed her eyes, expecting a peck on the cheek, instead he walked by like she was invisible. When she opened her eyes, he was sitting at a table, writing in his notebook. She fought to keep her emotions in check. He had to have seen me she thought, I was standing in the path to the table. She blushed with embarrassment when the boys giggled and hurried out of the library to tell their friends what they saw.

She was deciding what to do when Webster told her, "Don't take it personally, he's like that when he's working on a problem. The seed school marching band could practice here and he wouldn't notice. He's been like that since he was old enough to come here by himself."

She lifted her paws and said in a shaky voice, "I thought he saw me."

"He's like Sparky when he's working, totally focused on what he's doing," Webster said when he saw the look of disappointment on her face at being ignored.

"Not to me," she said angrily as she picked up her backpack. "Not today," she added as she hurried to the door. If she hoped to send a message to JR that she was upset at being ignored she failed, he hadn't heard a word she said.

JR looked up in surprise when Webster tapped him on the shoulder and whispered, "The library's closing. Leave your things where they are and come back in the morning."

It took a moment for him to return to the real world. He'd been searching for a more efficient way to store acorns. Using his formula, he could save a minimum of two square feet in underground storage areas so community members wouldn't have to dig so deep to prepare for winter. Or they could dig the normal depth and add more acorns.

"Sorry," he mumbled as he jammed papers in his briefcase. He'd reached the door when Webster told him, "Beck was here." JR didn't hear him, he almost had it. In his mind he pictured a three-dimensional shape, not a cylinder, more of a...

"Oh, my," someone said, "he didn't see me either."

He saw Beck's nestmates visiting in the Clearing. "I'm sorry, did you say..." He remembered Webster mentioning Beck came to the library. Or she was coming.

"Did you hear something?" The one with her asked.

"Not me," the nestmate said, glared at JR, and walked away.

JR stood in the Clearing trying to figure out what was going on. The bigger problem was, the shape he saw for storing acorns before leaving the library, was gone.

At his desk the next morning, Roscoe tried to concentrate on a letter from the COC, but his mind kept drifting back to the incident the night before. Violence was rare in Abner. Someone would get their feelings hurt by something someone said, but it usually ended with an apology. He rubbed the bump on the back of his head as he thought about the incident.

He had trouble believing Jarvis was guilty of something as complicated as breaking into Leander's office. He seldom spoke during a meeting and was usually the first to leave when it was over. Yet, after grabbing the hat and leaving the room, he hadn't been seen. There was no way he could be... he stopped in the middle of the thought when he saw movement out of the corner of his eye. He looked closer and saw someone he didn't recognize standing next to the door with his back to the wall. He brought a finger to his lips, telling Roscoe not to respond.

The door opened and Leander walked in.

Roscoe watched the stranger drop to the floor, crawl to the conference table, and crouch so only his eyes and the top of his head were visible. Leander stopped halfway to Roscoe's desk and said, "You've got to do better than that Finly, I saw you the moment I entered the room." Leander grabbed a chair from the conference table, moved it closer to Roscoe's desk, and sat down.

Finly, having been detected, came over and stood at attention behind him.

"There's nothing new to report on the missing files," Leander said with a sigh. He raised a paw, formed a fist, and wiggled it from side to side. Finly left and returned with two cups of walnut tea. He gave one to Leander and the other to Roscoe.

Roscoe asked, "Isn't he having one?"

Leander shook his head. "Not while on duty. I gave Megan the morning off, I don't want to drag her into this mess." Leander lifted a paw, pointed to his eyes, and Finly left the room to stand guard outside. Seeing the confused look on Roscoe's face, he explained, "He's an AIT, agent in training, still learning the ropes."

He took a sip of tea before continuing. "The thing that's puzzling is how the person was able to steal the files. They're kept in a locked cabinet in a room guarded twenty-four seven by our finest agents." He shook his head. "In spite of the safeguards they were taken and until the are found..." He raised his paws, letting Roscoe know the staff at the COC was working around the clock to replace the material the culprit took but it was slow going.

He was about to say something else when they heard a commotion on the platform and Darin burst in the room with Finly on his back. Leander said, "At ease Finly. You need to work on the choke hold, he's still conscious."

Darin stopped when he reached Roscoe's desk and said, "It's chaos at the post office. Mailboxes have been renumbered so no one is getting the right mail. Someone adjusted the controls on the sorting machine, letters are all over the place. Ferrel Jr. is working on it but…" He stopped when he saw Leander and asked, "What's he doing here?"

Leander walked to the window, looked out and said quietly, "So it begins."

Roscoe pulled a chair from the conference table so Darin could sit down but he was too keyed up to stay in one place.

Webster entered and, after eluding Finly's outreached arms said, "When I opened the library this morning, I discovered someone broke in during the night and dumped the card catalog on the floor. I have no idea which books are checked out or when they're due."

Leander tilted his head, Finly moved to the door and stood at parade rest. He turned to Webster and Darin and said, "An explanation is in order."

There was a knock on the door and Leander gestured for Finly to see who it was. He stepped outside, came back in, walked quickly to Leander and whispered in his ear. Leander nodded and told Roscoe, "Jarvis has been found."

"Where?" Roscoe asked in surprise.

"He said he was visiting a friend in the Community of Ben, lost track of time, and stayed overnight," Leander said through a skeptical laugh. "He refuses to name who he was with. If he's telling the truth, where's the travel request form he's required to fill out?" he said like the answer was obvious. "I think we've found our document thief Mr. Chairman."

Roscoe wasn't sure. Though new to the community, Jarvis wasn't that kind of person. Nothing suggested he could pull off something as complicated as overpowering two experienced agents and removing documents from a locked cabinet. He doubted he could find COC headquarters if you gave him a map and turn by turn instructions.

He remembered Megan saying someone requested a travel form. He went to the file cabinet, removed a folder, looked inside and found it was empty. He put it back, removed the one behind it and saw, along with a month's worth of meeting minutes, the travel request

Jarvis submitted. He put it in the correct folder, joined Leander at the window and said, "I have a problem."

"I would think so. If your secretary had..." Leander stopped when the door opened and Rupert, owner of the bowling alley entered, pushing a stranger in front of him.

Finly tried to tackle him, but Rupert stiff-armed him and continued to where Roscoe was standing.

"What's he doing here?" Leander asked, pointing at the stranger, not Rupert.

Roscoe shrugged. He had no idea who he was or why Rupert would bring him here.

"Sorry for interrupting your meeting but this guy has something to say," Rupert explained as he pushed the stranger closer to where Roscoe and Lothar were standing. The stranger looked at the floor, avoiding eye contact.

"So, a guy walks in a bowling alley, asks for a drink, and tells the bartender to hurry up, he doesn't have a moment to *spare*." Rupert chuckled. When the others didn't get it he said, "Sorry, a little bowling alley humor. Anyway, this deadbeat," he pointed to the stranger, "walked in my bowling alley, plopped a bag of seeds on the counter, and said the drinks were on him. I was suspicious. I know everyone in the community, but I've never seen this bozo before. I served him a drink and he opened up like a seven ten split."

"Opened up?" Roscoe didn't get it. It was hard to follow what Rupert was saying because the stranger had curled up on the floor and said he thought he was going to be sick.

"Spilled the beans. Let the cat out of the bag. His name is Mitch and said he got the seeds from," he pointed at Leander, "him."

"Me?" Leander said in surprise, "I've never seen him before in my life."

Rupert shook his head. "That really bugs me you know. What happened to integrity? Back in the day, if a guy did something wrong, he took responsibility for it." He turned to Leander and said, "I've seen guys like you at the bowling alley. They talk a good game but when push comes to shove, they fall apart like a cheap bowling pin."

Rupert turned to go, had a thought, pointed to Mitch, and said, "If you want, I'll stick around and keep an eye on him." Mitch had crawled to a corner of the room and was holding his head in his paws.

"What did you serve him?" Roscoe asked.

"I figured it was his last frame, so I gave him a *Gutter Ball*, the house special," Rupert said sheepishly.

"Believe me Roscoe I have no..." Leander said, pleading for Roscoe to understand.

"I have found, although a little rough around the edges, Rupert tells the truth, even when it works against him," Roscoe said with certainty.

"You'd take the word of the owner of a bowling alley and discount all that I have..." Then it was like Leander ran out of steam. He sat down and asked, "When did you figure it out?"

"The files were taken from your office. Nothing happened in our community until you arrived."

"I don't see how you could..."

"Blaming Jarvis who, to my knowledge, would have trouble opening a locked cabinet if you gave him a key," Roscoe said as he walked over and put a paw on top of the file cabinet. "You knew his travel request form was missing. I suppose that was the reason for giving Megan the day off. When I found it in another folder, I was sure it was you. As long as she's worked for the committee, she has never filed anything in the wrong place."

Leander took a deep breath, let it out and said in a voice barely above a whisper, "It's Lavinia."

"Lavinia?" Roscoe didn't understand. Before becoming Leander's life partner and moving away, Lavinia lived wrote the *Ask Lavinia* column for the Abner Echo.

"She buys things," Leander groaned. "Expensive things. She gets her nails trimmed and polished every week. Lately she's become hooked on imported nuts. I had a buyer for the files, so I gave the guards the night off and arranged for Mitch to break in and take them."

The door opened and members of the safety team entered. Leander figured when Roscoe stood with his back to the window it was the signal for help. He shook his head and said defiantly, "As a member of the COC, I have immunity. I only answer to the highly exalted chairman."

"They're not here to arrest you, they want to ask a few questions before filing a report." Roscoe pointed to Mitch who was stretched out on the floor, sleeping it off, and told Lester to, "Take him with you."

Leander knew friendship was important to Roscoe and he'd crossed the line. "I'm..." he started to say he was sorry for the trouble he'd caused but Roscoe had returned to the window, waiting for him to leave.

JR stood at the workbench in Sparky's lab, pushing a ball of twine from one paw to the other. Try as he might, nothing made sense. He couldn't remember what he was writing his paper on or what difference it made if he could. There were the comments of Beck's nestmate, he had no idea what that was about.

"An acorn for your thoughts," Sparky said. He recognized the signs, he felt the same way when Liz came into his life. He couldn't have told you what two plus two was if you gave him four guesses.

"It's nothing," JR sighed.

"It must be something, you've worn through a layer of twine. I'll take a wild guess it has something to do with Rebecca."

It took a moment for him to make the connection, Sparky was the only one who called her Rebecca. He reluctantly nodded it was. "I was at the library and carried some books from the reference section to the table where I was working, I guess I didn't see her."

"You guess?" Sparky asked, raising an eyebrow.

JR shrugged letting him know it wasn't on purpose.

Sparky put a paw on his shoulder and said, "Think of it as a problem. Person A is upset about something person B did. So, person B should..."

"See person A?" JR said hesitantly. Then with more enthusiasm, "Person B should see person A and apologize."

Sparky crossed the lab, opened the door and told him to, "Get going, you don't have a moment to lose."

"But it's raining," JR protested.

"Take my umbrella," Sparky said, handing it to him.

JR stood beneath Rebecca's nest. Rain beat against the umbrella and puddles of water formed around his feet. He called her name but wasn't sure she heard over the sound of rain drops hitting the leaves above her nest and the rumble of thunder in the distance.

He turned to go but stopped when she asked, "What are you doing here?" He looked up and saw her with her arms resting on the edge of the nest, glaring at him.

"I'm sorry. I... get like that, lost in my work and kind of..." JR hesitated, He hadn't had time to get the wording right.

She turned to her nestmate and asked, "Did you hear something? Or was it rain hitting a mud puddle?"

"Beck please, give me a chance to explain. I saw you but didn't see you. Does that make sense?" He was sure it didn't, he didn't understand it himself.

She waited. He was going to have to do better than that to change her mind. And no, it didn't make sense.

"When I'm working on a problem, I lose track of time. Forget to eat or sleep." He wasn't good at this. He was used to problems with one answer, not half a dozen.

"Me to," she said as she left her nest and climbed down the tree. "I can read for hours and be unaware of where I am or what's going on around me." When she reached the ground, she walked over, took the umbrella from him, and tossed it aside.

"We'll get wet," he said as she wrapped her arms around him, put her head on his chest and asked, "Do you have a problem with that?"

He looked in her beautiful blue eyes. shook his head and said, "I'm good."

Ferrel was chatting with friends in the Clearing when he saw Lester take Leander and Mitch to the safety training room to find out how they managed to steal the files. He waited until Roscoe closed the door to the meeting room and started up the path to his nest. He wasn't going there but wanted Ferrel to think he was.

"What's going on?" Ferrel asked when he caught up with him.

"Leander is here to check our first aid supplies," Roscoe said without stopping.

"Who's the guy with him?" Ferrel wasn't easily discouraged.

Roscoe shrugged, "An assistant from the COC."

Ferrel tried not to laugh; Roscoe couldn't tell a lie if the fate of the community hung in the balance. "I was at the bowling alley."

Roscoe kept going.

"His name is Mitch. Rupert took him outside, but I heard enough to know something is going on at the COC."

"Oh?" from Roscoe.

"If he's here to check our first aid supply, what was he doing in the meeting room?"

Roscoe didn't respond. He saw where this was going and knew Ferrel wouldn't stop until ` he had the whole story. He glanced at the position of the sun and said, "I'm late for a meeting with Chairman Ben," and hurried away.

"You can run but you can't hide," Ferrel shouted after him and decided he'd wait until Lester finished with Leander, then pump him for information.

Roscoe hurried down the path to Ben but had no intention of going there. He wanted to get to the COC and tell Highly Exalted Chairman Cletus what had gone on. If he heard it from Leander, it wouldn't resemble what actually happened.

Finly was perched on top of the big rock that separates the two communities. He was hiding behind the tree the safety training room is in and heard Roscoe tell Ferrel he was going to the community of Ben.

His mentor was in trouble, and he had to keep Roscoe from making things worse. He heard the sound of Roscoe's footsteps on the path and crouched down, out of sight. They covered this in the agent training manual, it was all about timing his jump with Roscoe's pace. He heard a foot hit the gravel in front of the rock, counted to three, and jumped.

Roscoe turned when he reached the big rock and took the path to the COC.

Finly was in the air, sailing toward the target when the target changed directions. He landed awkwardly, rolled across the path, and slammed into the trunk of a tree, knocking the breath from him. As he lay there, listening to Roscoe's footsteps grow fainter he wondered if he was cut out for the spy business.

UP, UP, AND AWAY

Harold looked up from the article he was reading in *Fountain Pen World* when he heard noise outside his office in the security room. He opened the door and found the managers standing in the hallway, talking to one another.

"Can I help you?" he asked.

"I don't think so." "Not us." "We're good." They said at the same time.

"Why are you here?" Harold asked, confused by their response.

Before they could answer, Dawson hurried down the stairs from the second floor, pointed to the security room and told them to, "Go inside, Big G is waiting." When they did it was so crowded, Dawson had to squeeze by them to get to the wall where the monitors are located. He pointed to one, hit enter on the keyboard, and they found they were looking at the street in front of *The Big G Grocery and Otis Tharp Fountain Pen Museum.*

The door to the museum opened and a smiling Big G walked down the front steps. He stopped when he reached the sidewalk, looked at the security camera above the door and announced, "It's a new day in Centerline. Starting with a fruit stand downtown, Big G Grocery has grown to five stores, two in the city and three in the suburbs. An accomplishment like that doesn't happen by accident, it takes careful planning and total commitment."

A car horn honked, and the driver asked if he'd escaped from the loony bin, standing on the sidewalk, talking to a building. Big G waved, said, "Good morning. Have a nice day," and turned back to the camera. A woman walking a dog went behind him, the dog went in front. It took a moment for her to untangle the leash that had wrapped around Big G's legs. She apologized. Big G patted the dog and told her, "No problem."

He strolled down the sidewalk to the parking lot like he didn't have a care in the world. The camera on the front of the building followed him until he was out of range and the one on the side picked him up. The managers switched from watching one monitor to another. As he walked toward the field in back of the museum a car pulled alongside him. The driver rolled down a window and asked if he could validate his parking ticket or if he had to go inside to do it.

Big G pointed to the museum, said, "In there," thanked him for his business, and gave him a coupon for ten percent off anything in the dairy section at a Big G grocery store.

He stopped when he reached the edge of the field, turned toward the camera and said, "At my high school graduation the guest speaker challenged our class to dream big. I don't know about the others, but I took him seriously and am asking you to imagine...." his voice was drowned out by the sound of an ambulance going by, the siren blaring. When it was gone, he continued unfazed, "...where I am standing today." He moved toward the dumpster and the camera on the back of the building took over. He pointed to the field and said, "You see a vacant lot, but I see," he pointed to a sign stuck in the ground that announced it was the *Future Home of the Big G International Heliport."*

The managers clapped and though they knew Big G couldn't hear them, shouted their approval.

Harold wondered how it could be called international, he doubted a helicopter could make it to either coast, let alone out of the country.

Big G continued. "You're probably wondering why someone would build a heliport in the heart of the city. Well, I'll tell you. It takes an hour to drive to the airport on a good day. Add a little snow, throw in a fender bender..." He didn't finish, anyone who'd made the trip knew the rest. Churning stomachs as their gas gage approached empty and the fear of missing a flight turned a pleasant drive in the country into a nightmare.

"It takes fifteen minutes in a helicopter because the pilot won't encounter congested highways and treacherous driving conditions. They'll see nothing but blue skies and green lights." Big G smiled.

So did the managers.

"The heliport will be built where I'm standing. The first floor of the museum will serve as the terminal where tickets are sold, and passengers wait for their flight. At the far end of the field, extending into the woods, a hanger will serve as a temporary control tower and provide space for overnight storage. A mechanic will be on duty twenty-four seven to service the helicopters and make repairs."

He looked at the camera and said, "If you're watching Finebender, your concern for getting a permit to remove part of the woods is touching but unnecessary because," he paused, before saying, "I own it. Or will when Victoria Climber defeats Mayor Blanton in the November election."

Those watching in Harold's office heard a whomp, whomp sound and watched a helicopter touch down on the field. Debris was yanked from the ground, trash pulled from the dumpster, and the hair on Big G's head swirled, exposing the bald spot he kept covered with a comb-over.

He shouted over the noise of the whirling helicopter blades, "I'll have more to say when I'm back in the office but my ride to the airport is here." He climbed on board, buckled the seat belt, and stuck a thumb in the air as the helicopter rose from the field and flew out of camera range.

The silence in Harold's office was followed by shouts of praise for their boss and his vision for the future. As they filed out of the room, Harold stayed behind, looking at the monitor showing the field and wondered if the squirrels would survive another attack on their home.

Norman was bored. He had a little longer to go before his replacement arrived and, other than recording in the logbook a human was walking in the field behind Seed Man's building, nothing unusual had happened. To kill time, he'd gathered a paw full of acorns and threw them at the trunk of a tree. When he'd thrown the last one, he went to get them and missed the helicopter dropping to the ground and going back up.

Lothar, the one who set up the guard schedule, heard the noise and ran through the woods as fast as his bad knee would allow to find out what was going on.

When he reached Norman he asked, "What was that?" while catching his breath.

Norman didn't know what he was talking about. One of the acorns he'd thrown went deeper in the woods than the others. He found it and returned to his post moments before Lothar arrived. He shrugged he didn't know what he was talking about.

"The noise. The change in air pressure. Stuff blowing all over the place." Lothar couldn't believe Norman missed it, he was in the middle of woods and heard it.

"I was here but..." Norman lifted his paws, letting him know he hadn't seen or heard anything unusual.

"I'll expect a full report of the incident when your replacement arrives," Lothar growled and started back through the woods.

"Sure. No problem," Norman said but wondered how he could write a report about something that didn't happen.

While that was going on at the edge of the woods, Beck and JR stood on the platform outside the meeting room. "You're sure about this?" she asked.

JR took her paw in his and told her, "Absolutely." He had a great relationship with his father. Growing up they talked about everything. He was the one who encouraged him to pursue his interest in science although it meant spending more time with Sparky than him. In spite of that, he had a lump in his throat thinking about telling his father about their plans to be joined. He loved Beck, there was no question about it and knew she felt the same about him.

He was about to knock on the door when Lothar growled, "Out of my way," pushed passed him, entered the room, and shouted, "Something has to be done!" before slamming the door.

"What now?" Beck asked.

"We wait," JR said and pointed to *Out On A Limb*. "How about a nut cake and walnut tea. We'll get a table by a window and come back when Lothar leaves." He was used to members of the community taking advantage of his father's open-door policy. He couldn't count the number of times he'd experienced the same thing while growing up.

"We can spend the time writing our vows," Beck said.

"Great," JR replied, not as enthused about the idea as she was.

Harold sat at his desk, trying to grasp the significance of Big G's plan to transform the field into a heliport. He was sure putting it this close to downtown Centerline violated dozens of laws. Everything from noise pollution to danger for those living in the flight path. Fuel would have to be stored someplace which brought another set of problems. And, with helicopters landing and taking off all hours of the day, the tranquil life of the squirrels in what would be left of the woods would become a nightmare.

The thing that popped up every time he thought about the difficulties Big G faced constructing the heliport was his comment about owning the woods when Victoria became mayor. That seemed unlikely. The latest poll taken by *Centerline Morning* said the chance of her winning fell somewhere between slim and none. She owned a company named *Victoria Paves* that resurfaced parking lots and survived in a rough and tumble business by being as aggressive and underhanded as her competitors.

The only reason he knew about her was a few years ago she submitted a bid for work on the museum parking lot. He threw it out when he got a call from a friend who said she was the low bidder to resurface his parking lot then gouged him for extras. "You want a smooth surface?" she'd ask, shake her head and say, "That's going to cost you."

So far, her campaign consisted of attacking Mayor Blanton's character, she'd said nothing about her vision for the city. She was a large woman and blunt to the point of being rude. He doubted she knew how a city was organized or what the duties of the mayor were.

He felt restless so he got up and walked around the room. He turned when he reached Officer Gardner's equipment locker and was on the way back to his desk when he glanced at the monitor showing the field where Big G planned to build the heliport. He looked closer and saw a squirrel standing at the edge of the woods with an arm in the air. If he weren't a squirrel enthusiast, he would have missed it.

Curious, he left his office, stopped by the storage room to pick up the bag of seeds he kept there for filling the feeder he hung in the woods, then stepped outside. He was relieved when he saw the squirrel hadn't moved from the spot by the tree.

He was about to enter the woods when the squirrel lowered his arm and started down a path only visible to a creature his size. Harold followed and soon was standing near a small pond. He remembered it from the pictures Lloyd Brewster took of the Big G worker dumping toxic waste.

The squirrel led him around the pond to a place where the grass was pushed down like someone had been walking around. He reached down, picked something up and held it at arm's length. Harold saw he was holding the stub of a cigar. The squirrel moved a few feet and pulled the grass aside to reveal indentations made by a heavyset person wearing work boots.

It took Harold a moment to put things together. Was his guide telling him a meeting took place here? He was sure the cigar belonged to Big G. Were the impressions in the ground made by Victoria Climber? It was a perfect place to meet, away from prying eyes and close to a seldom used road, she could arrive and depart without being seen.

The problem was it was all circumstantial. The footprints could belong to anyone. Big G wasn't the only one who bought that brand of cigar. He could do a DNA test on it but that would be expensive and wouldn't prove anything sinister was going on, Big G was free to walk in the woods if he wanted. But, with the help of the squirrel, he'd made a connection that might come in handy.

He looked to see if the squirrel had more evidence, but it was gone.

As he walked back to the museum, he saw Big G standing by the dumpster, his hands on his hips and a scowl on his face. When he was close enough to hear, Big G asked, "Where have you been?"

Harold held up the bag of seeds. "I was filling the feeder I put in the woods the day the museum opened. I find it relaxing to get out of the office for a few minutes."

"Enjoy it while you can because after the election, the trees will be gone. I need the space for a hanger and a fuel storage area."

"The woods are lovely this time of year, especially around the pond by Timberline Drive. Have you been there?" He hoped Big G got the message he was aware of the secret meeting that took place there. He removed the cigar butt from his pocket and held it long enough for Big G to see it before tossing it in the dumpster.

Big G became suspicious when Harold mentioned the pond. "What's that supposed to mean?" he growled. When Harold didn't answer, he walked to the back door of the museum, punched a number on the electronic keypad, and hurried to his office, he had a phone call to make.

JR saw the meeting room door open and Lothar leave. He told Beck his dad was available. They were halfway across the Clearing when Lester ran up the steps, entered the room, and closed the door.

Beck saw the disappointment on JR's face and suggested they try again tomorrow. He took her paws in his and apologized for the delay.

She suggested taking a walk would help and he agreed.

Inside the meeting room Lester told Roscoe about taking Seed Man to the pond and showing him what the safety team had found. He asked if he'd heard about Dexter finding a sign with human markings on it near the box where humans put trash. Roscoe told him Webster was translating it and promised to explain what it said as soon as he finished.

"I wonder what that's about," Officer Gardner said and pointed to the monitor connected to the camera aimed at the parking lot.

"What's going on?" Harold asked, as he left his desk and moved closer to the wall of monitors. He saw Big G standing next to a large woman wearing jeans, a denim shirt, scuffed work boots, and a hard hat. Behind them, parked at an angle and taking up three spaces, was a truck with *Victoria Paves* painted on the side. She appeared to be an inch or two taller than Big G but she was wearing a hardhat, so it was hard to tell.

Big G pointed to a place on the pavement. She ran the toe of her boot over it and sprayed it with white paint. What looked to someone driving by like the owner of the museum talking to a contractor about resurfacing the parking lot, was actually an emergency meeting called by Big G after his encounter with Harold.

"I'm telling you, he's on to us," Big G held the end of the tape while Victoria wrote something in her notebook.

"What makes you think that?" she asked as she moved to a new location.

"He came back from the woods, mentioned the road in back of the pond, and tossed a cigar butt in the dumpster," Big G said nervously.

"So?" she said.

"It wasn't so much what he said but the way he said it. Like, I know what went on out there and you won't get away with it."

"Relax G Man. If he causes trouble my boys will teach him to keep his nose out of your business. But it won't come to that. When the press hears what Mayor Blanton's been up to while in office, it'll be over before the polls open."

Big G's managers wouldn't recognize their boss if they saw him. The belligerent, larger than life personality they were used to, had been replaced by one that was mild mannered, almost timid. He had an, I wish I'd never allowed himself to be dragged into this, look on his face. He'd allowed his desire to get even with Harold and cut down the trees in his precious woods to overpower his common sense.

Victoria rolled up the tape and put it and her notebook in the cab of the truck. She climbed in but before closing the door said, "While I'm holding a press conference tomorrow at the *Great Mall of Centerline*, a concerned citizen will call the editor of *Centerline Morning* and tell him about the mayor's latest shenanigans."

Big G knew better than ask but he couldn't help himself. "Who's making the call?"

She grinned, started the truck, handed him a piece of paper and said, "That's where you come in G Man. If you want to play you've got to pay," then gunned the motor and was gone.

A quick glance at the paper revealed a list of items. The first said the mayor was consorting with lobbyists and receiving kickbacks for voting their way on certain issues. All were rumors that had been investigated and proven false. He felt he was between a rock and a hard place. The rock was, he knew the accusations against the mayor were false, made up by Victoria and her staff. The hard place was, if he didn't make the call, the crew she said would rough Harold up, knew where he worked.

Early the next morning, JR and Beck walked down the path to the Clearing. They planned to be the first in line to see his father. They opened the door to the meeting room and found Megan at her desk, sorting mail. She smiled when she saw them and, after exchanging greetings, asked what they were doing here so early.

JR said they would like to have a few minutes with his father.

She frowned, said she was sorry, he'd been called to an emergency meeting at COC headquarters and wouldn't be back until the afternoon.

"Maybe then?" JR asked, hopefully.

"He'll be gone all morning, so his schedule is backed up." She glanced at the calendar on the wall behind her desk. "He's free this evening but that could change depending on how things go at the COC, it may require a committee meeting. How about this time next week?" Then, "No, wait, I forgot about the committee retreat."

JR shrugged thinking the meeting room wasn't the best place to have a discussion with his father. He'd talk to him tonight at home but after the day he'd had, who knew what kind of mood he'd be in.

The election was less than a month away and Harold was afraid Mayor Blanton was going to get blindsided by a last-ditch attack from Victoria Climber. From the way Big G was acting, Harold was sure he was in over his head. There was the secret meeting in the woods, then acting like they were estimating the cost to repave the parking lot. On top of that, Big G hadn't called a meeting to report on progress of the heliport project since the roll out a month ago.

Several times he'd heard someone breathing when he was on the phone arranging tours for fountain pen enthusiasts. It wasn't unusual for Dawson to enter his office, look around to make sure he was alone, then leave without saying anything.

He was frustrated he couldn't do something as simple as call home without someone listening to his conversation when he had an idea. He'd flip it around and change it from call home to call from home. And the best thing was, he wouldn't be doing it, Thelma would.

"Do what now?" she asked, not sure she heard him over the dishes he was clanking together before putting them in the dishwasher. He didn't think Big G had bugged their house but wasn't taking any chances. He turned the water in the sink on and said, "Call Traci Kline at *Centerline Morning*. But not from here."

She laughed. "Me? Call a reporter at the newspaper? You can't be serious." Traci Kline wrote the article that told her readers she'd been arrested for reckless driving. She was the last person she wanted to talk to.

As he opened and closed drawers taking out pans and putting them back, he explained what was going on and why she couldn't use the home phone.

"What phone should I use?" she asked then shook her head, anticipating what he was going to say. "No, no, no. Not the one at Rosie's." She'd been there before and was uncomfortable driving through that part of town, afraid one of her friends would see her. Going there a second time increased the chance they would.

"Big G won't be listening on Rosie's phone. Federal agents might but calling a newspaper reporter will fly under their radar," Harold told her, trying to make it sound like it was no big deal.

Thelma had met Mayor Blanton a few times. His wife Betty was a member of the Centerline chapter of *Women Who Wear Gray Shoes*.

Before saying she'd do it, she made Harold agree to switch cars, lessening the chance someone recognizing her.

It was close to noon when she pulled in the parking lot at Rosie's. The two men she'd seen the last time she was here were standing by the entrance. Like before, one opened the door and welcomed her to Rosie's. She was looking for the pay phone when a voice from a booth at the back of the restaurant said, "Mrs. F, are youse here for lunch?" She looked around, not sure what to say. She hadn't expected to be greeted by Vinny Bling. The last time she was here, Rosie said he didn't come in on Tuesdays. "No, I, ah, need to make a phone call."

"Have youse had an accident? Car trouble? I'll get the boys to..." he waited to hear what brought her to Rosie's.

"It's personal A rather delicate matter," she said the first thing that popped in her mind.

Vinny tilted his head, grinned, and asked, "Who's the lucky guy?"

"What? No. It's not...," she was embarrassed he thought she was having an affair.

Vinny stepped back, raised his hands and said, "Hey, what's said at Rosie's stays at Rosie's. But youse don't need to pay for the call, use the phone on the counter where Rosie gets orders for takeout." He walked with her to the phone, lifted the handset, and handed it to her.

She thanked him and waited until he returned to his booth before dialing *Centerline Morning* and asking for Traci Kline. When she finished delivering the message, she hung up, thanked Rosie for the use of his phone, waved goodbye to Vinny and left, happy to have the ordeal over and done with.

As she pulled out of the parking lot one of the men outside the restaurant opened the door and gave Vinny the thumbs up sign, letting him know she'd gone.

Vinny walked over, pressed play on the answering machine and listened as Thelma explained to Traci Kline that Victoria Climber was about to leak a memo accusing Mayor Blanton of taking money under the table for ignoring code violations on a building under construction. If she would join the ten o'clock tour at the *Big G*

Grocery and Otis Tharp Fountain Pen Museum tomorrow, Harold would fill in the details.

Vinny went back to his booth where Bruno was waiting. Mayor Blanton was seeking his second term in office, to throw a new person in now would destroy all the work he'd done. Victoria would replace department managers and the chief of police, all had received gifts and gone on vacations at his expense. He wasn't about to let that happen.

He motioned for Bruno to lean closer and explained in a whisper, "Here's what I have in mind." When he finished, Bruno nodded, slipped out of the booth, and left, taking the men at the door with him.

Harold waited in the Grand Hall for a group to form before starting the ten o'clock tour of the museum. Among them was Traci Kline. At Thelma's suggestion she'd changed her appearance since the last time she was there. She wore jeans, sneakers, and a Centerline Clippers sweatshirt. They were moving to the *Presidential Pens Room* when Dawson hurried down the hall, stopped Harold and asked, "What's going on?"

"It's the morning tour. There's one at ten and two on weekdays," Harold explained as he followed the last tour member into the room.

"I know that, what I'm asking is why are you leading it?" Dawson asked suspiciously.

"My volunteers quit when Big G insisted they work sales at his grocery stores into their presentation. Besides, I enjoy doing it."

"Who's she?" Dawson asked, pointing to a woman at the front of the group.

"Check the list on the counter near the entrance, their names are listed under *Morning Tour*," Harold said as he stepped in the room.

"She looks familiar," Dawson said as he pushed through the group who resisted, thinking he was trying to cut in front of them to get closer to the display case. To Harold's relief he walked past Traci Kline to an older woman at the front. "Miss," he said tapping her shoulder. When she didn't respond he took her arm, turned her around, stepped back in surprise and said, "Mother?"

"Yes dear. You said I should see where you work." She pointed in Harold's direction and said, "The nice man over there invited me."

"If you'd let me know you were coming, I would have…" Dawson sputtered, trying to come to grips with his mother showing up unannounced.

"Quiet, dear. I can't hear what the tour guide is saying," she said in a whisper and turned to face Harold.

Harold took advantage of the confusion caused by Dawson and his mother to slip a note inside the brochure Tracie picked up describing Otis Tharp's passion for fountain pens. She nodded, letting him know she got it.

The tour ended back at the check-in desk. Several remained, asking questions about what they saw. While answering them, Harold saw Traci hurry down the front steps and hop in a cab waiting at the curb.

When the last guest left, Harold took Dawson's mother to his office on the first floor.

That afternoon, Harold walked to his car wondering what Traci Kline would do with the information he gave her, so he didn't notice the scruffy looking guy standing by the dumpster. "You Harold?" he asked in a raspy voice and took a step toward him.

"Yes," Harold answered. He became concerned when he saw *Victoria Paves* printed above the pocket of his shirt. "How can I…" He stopped when he heard a car door close and someone holler, "Hey Mr. F, you got a minute?" He was relieved when he saw Bruno walking toward him.

"Get in line buddy, I was here first," the one who stopped Harold said and smacked a fist in the palm of his hand, letting Bruno know he was serious.

Unfazed by the man's threats, Bruno said, "First, I ain't your buddy. And second, I don't see no line."

Bruno put an arm around Harold's shoulders and walked with him to his car. He didn't slow down when he heard, "Hey, what do you think you're…" from the one Victoria sent to teach Harold to mind his own business. The question was followed by the sound of something heavy hitting the bottom of the dumpster.

"Have a good evening," Bruno said and waited until Harold was safely out of the parking lot before asking, "We good here boys?"

One of the men who usually stood at the door to Rosie's raised a thumb as he walked away from the dumpster. The other chuckled and said, "Your buddy might get wet, it looks like it could rain," as he got in the backseat of Bruno's car and closed the door.

Reporters from various news outlets gathered in a corner of the parking lot at the *Great Mall of Centerline*. They waited past the time announced for the press conference and wondered if they were in the right place. They were about to leave when a pickup truck turned off the street and drove toward them. It skidded to a stop and Victoria Climber climbed out.

She was dressed the way she was the day she met with Big G in the parking lot, jeans, a denim shirt, and work boots. "Good afternoon," she said as she walked toward them. "Sorry for running late but unlike my opponent in this election, I have to work for a living. He says being the owner of a paving company is different than running a city, but some things are the same. Like being honest and playing by the rules. I mention that because I have evidence that proves Mayor Blanton has been playing fast and loose with..."

She raised her voice to be heard over the sound of a police siren getting closer. One of the reporters raised a hand, identified herself as Traci Kline of *Centerline Morning* and asked. "What happened to the sign on your truck?"

Victoria looked and instead of *Victoria Paves* someone had changed it to *Victoria Caves*. "I don't... I didn't..." While she struggled to explain the change in the sign, a police car pulled in front of her truck, blocking any chance of her leaving. An officer got out and told her mall security called about a demonstration in the parking lot.

Victoria dropped the humble, I'm just a working stiff trying to make a living attitude and shifted to attack mode. "As a tax paying citizen, I have the right to..."

"Show me your permit to hold a press conference here and I'll leave you to it. Otherwise, this looks like an unruly mob looking for trouble," the officer explained.

Victoria said she called city hall about a permit and was told she didn't need one.

"Who'd you talk to?" the officer asked, ready to write down the name.

"Bob. Or Rob, I don't remember," Victoria said and waved a hand, saying with the gesture, who has time to keep track of stuff like that when you're in the middle of a political campaign?

"Ms. Climber, there are four clerks at city hall, none named Bob. I'm going to need a name because whoever said you didn't need a permit gave you bad information." He turned to the reporters and said, "The shows over folks, I suggest you move along."

Victoria told the reporters to, "Stay where you are. When you hear what's going on at city hall," is as far as she got before the officer placed a hand on her arm, moving her toward the police car. She pushed his hand away and said angrily, "Keep your paws off me buster, I've decked bigger men than you."

The officer spoke as he wrote on his notepad, "Unlawful assembly. Resisting arrest."

"Your truck," one of the reporters said, pointing at it.

"What about it?" Victoria grunted all sign of civility gone.

"It just tilted to one side," the reporter said in alarm.

Victoria looked and saw the back tire on the driver's side was flat. She glared at the reporters and yelled, "If I find out one of you two-bit hacks had anything to do with this, so help me I'll..." as the officer struggled to get her in the backseat of the patrol car.

Bruno waited until the reporters were gone before pulling out of a parking place and followed the signs to the exit.

Roscoe was back from meeting with the COC and on his way to the meeting room when he saw Beck and JR walking toward him, holding paws. He waved and as they got closer said, "Megan said you wanted to talk to me. I've got some time before the next meeting."

"We do," JR said, then changed it to, "did."

Roscoe noticed the difference and asked, "What's going on?"

"We're joined," Beck said before checking with JR to see if it was okay to tell him.

"Joined?" Roscoe said in surprise. "Where? How?"

"Chairman Ben performed the ceremony this morning," JR said, putting an arm around Beck.

"You should have said something. I would have been..." Roscoe sounded hurt they hadn't asked him to perform the ceremony. He knew Penny Sue would be upset when she found out.

JR choose not to mention they tried a couple of times, but he'd been tied up with committee business. Instead, he said, "We didn't want to make a big deal..." Before he could finish, Megan opened the door to the meeting room and hollered, "I'm glad I caught you. Penny is in labor. Doc said the baby is due any moment."

"We'll talk about this later, I have to go," Roscoe said over his shoulder as he hurried away.

JR and Beck agreed they'd done the right thing. In a few days he'd return to the science academy, and she'd start her second semester at seed school. They'd have a reception during spring break. They had was just enough time for a quick honeymoon at *Squirrels Of Fun* amusement park.

Mayor Blanton won in a landslide. Shortly after the disastrous press conference in the shopping center parking lot, Victoria's accountant, after being granted immunity, explained to the authorities she cooked the books, making more money than appeared on her tax form.

Accompanying Traci Kline's article about Victoria's attempt to buy the election, was a picture of her and other inmates paving the parking lot at city hall.

Big G learned he wasn't the only one she'd promised to sell the woods to. Everyone from an investment group to the CEO of a lumber company claimed she promised to sell it to them for a hefty contribution to her campaign.

The director of the Centerline Parks and Recreation Department swore under oath she knew nothing about the deals Victoria made. To make sure others weren't taken advantage of in future elections, she issued a press release stating the wooded areas in the city were not for sale, they were an important part of Mayor Blanton's *Green Side Up* environmental program.

The day after the election Harold drove to his parking place and was surprised to find there were no cars in the lot, he was usually the last to arrive. Big G demanded his managers arrive at the crack of dawn and stay until dark. On the way to his office, he noticed the museum was unusually quiet. He found Officer Gardner standing at the front door, looking out at the street.

"Where is everyone?" he asked after joining him. Normally department managers were rushing around, trying to carry out Big G's ideas to increase sales.

"Beats me," Officer Gardner said and handed him a note he found under the door of the security room when he arrived for work. It was a request from Big G to put his things in a box and keep it in the storage room until he sent a forwarding address.

Officer Gardner asked Harold if he needed help moving back to his office on the second floor. Harold accepted the offer but suggested before getting started they go to *Penultimate* for a cup of coffee and talk about all that had gone on since Big G showed up.

Webster finally figured out what the sign Dexter gave him said. Someone named Heliport was building a home in the field between Seed Man's building and the woods. He left the library, stopped the first committee member he saw, and told him to call a meeting so he could explain what the sign said.

The committee member told Webster he'd have to wait, "Doc says Penny and Ferrel Jr's baby could come any moment."

Like most expecting parents, Penny and Ferrel Jr. had searched family records and looked through books at the library for an appropriate name for their first child. They wanted it to be one that embodied kindness and concern for the welfare of others.

Late that night the population of the Community of Abner increased by one as the new parents welcomed their son Sam into the world. That was as close as they good get without actually naming him Seed Man.

Printed in the United States
by Baker & Taylor Publisher Services